The Qarma Group

By Adrian Jones

The Qarma Group

By Adrian Jones © 2024

Dedication

This book is a tribute to the fallen revolutionaries across the country which have fought and died so that we may douce the wild fires of systematic oppression.

Preface

An Introduction Past Due

In the land of capitalism where the lobbyist rule politics and classes are determined by financial status, tension among the have nots have reached a point of rebellion against the very system that has been designed to oppress them from the beginning. Tools like religion, entertainment, media, and other forms of deception have been established to maintain control of the masses for centuries. The media desensitizes the people with immoral behavior, violence, and social issues.

The foot soldiers of the system, known as the local police department, have waged war on minorities in every major city across the country. Racial profiling has become the source of probable cause to use deadly force when stopped for something as simple as a traffic violation. Entities of peace and justice have emerged from the gun powder hovering in the air of the Black communities. Though the hood is no stranger to police brutality, the level of police involved shootings have more than tripled over time.

This ideology has been a never-ending cycle due to a lack of history of ourselves, education, and ambition to pursue our goals. The pawns of entertainment whether in the music industry, motion pictures, or reality shows continue to mold the cultural fabric of our society. The message is all but productive to the growth and development of the people. The hip-hop culture has become all about glamour, drug trafficking, genocide, and material things. This false sense of reality is alluring to the people of poverty, therefore, enhancing the criminal element. Within the public schools, false history is being taught within an environment of extreme ignorance. It remains clear that the gap between prosperity and our current state remains distant.

This novel is about a family located in one of the worst cities in this nation, who have taken on the responsibility to level the playing field against a corrupt system in our country. Though we have a long way to go towards freedom and justice within our society, we should all start by enlightening ourselves, as well as our children, to what really takes place behind the scenes of what we call *the land of the free*. Maybe as a community, it's time for us to save ourselves instead of waiting for someone *or something* to do it for us.

What good is life if we choose to do nothing to preserve it? What good are our minds if we choose to indoctrinate it with religious spook stories? What good is free will if we have no cause?

Well, this family is down for the sacrifice. This family knows what it will take to start the renaissance. This family proves the old saying to be true: where there's a will, there's a way…

Table of Contents

Chapter 1

Althia was standing in the vestibule, while Uncle D and Focus sat on the steps with Don. I was racing my Big Wheel up and down the street with my buddy, Dominic, but we called him "Nicci Boy". He was a classic east side kid, extremely dark skinned, nappy head, and wore hand-me-down clothes. He lived six doors up from us with his older brother, E, and their mother, Ms. Donna.

Nicci and I were the same age and so were E and Don. Behind our houses was a huge cemetery. All the kids would play hide and seek there at night. The undertaker knew my family well. There was a group home on the corner of Luzerne and Federal. There were about twelve kids who lived there. Every time we played WWF, they would smell like dumpsters in the summer.

Althia called me to come in at 8 pm. Nicci and I parted ways, destined to kick it again tomorrow. When I walked up the steps, Uncle D grabbed my Big Wheel and followed the rest of us inside. Bella was studying her Bible in the living room. Don and I made our way upstairs to wash our hands after Bella instructed us to. Uncle D and Focus went into the kitchen with my mother and took a seat at the table. Don and I joined them shortly after. Bella came into the kitchen, made herself a plate and sat with us. Bella always had intimate talks with us about God and this was one of those moments.

"How are you boys?"

"We're good," Don replied.

I just nodded and bit a chunk off my porkchop. She then asked, "I want you boys to tell me about faith and what you think it means to you?"

Don answered, "Faith is for God, right?"

"Yes, as well as other things such as situations, circumstances, or a certain outcome that you may hope for."

Don asked, "Do you have faith, Bella?"

"Yes I do, Don. I have an extraordinary amount in the both of you. August, I want you to listen while I explain to you boys what faith is, alright?" We nodded.

"I want you to always hold on to my words for they will make more sense as you get older, okay my loves?"

We chimed in together, "Yes Bella."

"Every time you boys see me, my head is buried in the Bible. Every time I speak, it involves God and every time I find myself in difficult situations, I pray. The reason I do these things is because of my belief in Him and the outcome of past experiences. I wasn't always the person that I am now, and I owe it all to God."

When we got upstairs, I went into our room while Don went into the bathroom to run our bathwater. Thia made her way up to us and told Don to come in the room so she could speak to us. She sat us both down on the bottom bunk and crouched in front of us.

Thia was twenty-four years old at the time and painfully mean to anyone she came across. Everyone knew she meant well but the truth is her childhood turned her into something even she couldn't identify. I've never seen her cry, but I've seen her make other people cry, especially us. She was very physical when expressing herself. Thia would whip us just as easily as taking a breath. All and all, she made sure that we put our family first no matter what and till this day, that very concept is what kept us solid.

Chapter 2

The next two years came swiftly. Growing up on the east side made a couple of seven-year-olds immune to gunfire. We could even tell you what kind of gun was being used from ten blocks away. Baltimore was becoming a warzone, thanks to the local heroin cartels over territory.

My brother was playing ball in his spare time, and he was "nice" for a 12-year-old. The hustlers in the hood would side bet on him then split the profits with him.

Basketball was Don's way of escaping our environment, but Nicci and I embraced the neighborhood bullshit. My house became a haven of secrets. Focus, Thia, and my uncle were always under the radar of the public. They never dressed flashy, and went to clubs, parties or events.

The hustlers pulled up in Saab's SC Lex coups and 500 Benz. Uncle D and Focus had an emerald green "67" Chevelle. Bella kept Don and I in church every Sunday and she grew more aggressive with her Bible lessons as the times grew more dangerous within the city.

Regardless of how I felt or what I believed, nothing could've prepared me for what I had seen on the spring break of '94. It was a seventy-eight-degree day in April. Nicci Boy and I were on my front stoop pitching quarters. Don was at the court while Bella sat on the stoop next door with Ms. Flemings.

While we gambled, Nicc asked, "August, what do you want to be when you grow up?"

I responded without a second thought, "Batman!"

He laughed before he asked why. I said, "Because he doesn't have any powers and he still does what he wants, plus he's rich."

"Well, I just want to survive, August."

"What do you mean Nicc?"

"I don't want to die, August!"

"Me either, that's why I-ma be a superhero."

"We can't be them August; this is the real world and we gotta promise to stick together."

"I'm with you Nicc, let's stick together."

While we were making our pact, my mother's friend, Mr. Phil, pulled up and parked across the street in his white Jaguar. When he got out, he spoke to Bella and started towards us. He owned the record store across the street, and he would let us run wild in it all day. He held his fist out and gave us a pound.

"Wassup lil men?"

"Just chillin'," I replied.

"You know, pitching quarters leads to shooting dice, right?" We both grew quiet hoping that we would become invisible somehow.

"Did you hear me, boys?"

We realized that being invisible didn't work so we answered, "Yes sir."

"Well, if you know better, then do better boys." We agreed. "I see both of y'all have the same Nickelodeon shirts and watches on."

"We love Nickelodeon, that's all we watch Mr. Phil," Nicci said.

"Just stay kids as long as you can, you got it boys?"

He stuck his fist out again and gave us both a hard pound. Afterward, he stepped off towards the street and then looked back to let me know to tell Thia he needed to speak with her. He always wore shades and a gold watch on his left wrist. He always dressed as if he was going to a ball or something. Thia was always in his store and had keys to it too.

Don appeared out of nowhere. He was sweating profusely as he pulled out a pocket full of money and smacked us both with it.

"Y'all suckers need to get y'all weight up and get some money."

I replied, "We're seven years old dumbass!"

Nicci laughed, then Don put me in the L and tried to choke me out. Thia came out of nowhere and put him in a chokehold. Don released me immediately.

She didn't like us fighting each other, and she made it clear right then. He was gasping and kicking while she was talking to him.

"Are you a coward Don?" She loosened her grip a bit so he could speak.

"No Thia."

"Then why do you prey on the weak?" Her tone was cross.

"We were playing Thia."

"Don't lie, he was telling you to stop. What did I tell you about fighting ya family?"

"We can't win."

"That's right, so why don't we go upstairs so I can explain this to you the hard way. You can also explain where you got this money from and how it will contribute to the bills in this bitch!"

Thia let him go and he headed in the house. Thia gave me and Nicc kisses on our foreheads then punched Nicc in his chest for not helping me. Thia didn't care that she wasn't Nicci's mama.

"Nicci Boy, never let anyone hurt ya people, I don't care who it is, ok?!"

"Yes Ms. Thia."

She instructed me to stay on the porch until she came back downstairs. Thia went into the house to crucify Don.

While we were waiting on the porch, I could hear Don wailing and I was glad it wasn't me but sad for my brother gettin' torn up by Althia. Ms. Donna called Nicci in the house, so after we gave each other a farewell pound, that left me alone.

The neighborhood was alive that day. I remember guys hanging across the street in front of Phil's record shop listening to an endless playlist of oldies. Others were selling candy apples to the kids.

Finally, I turned my attention to the bar on the corner of Milton Avenue. That's where all the hustlers and hood stars hung out. They dressed the best but never went anywhere. Their cars were lined up in a row along the bus stop.

Suddenly, Uncle D and Focus pulled up in front of the house. Uncle D jumped out of the passenger's seat and gave Focus a pound. He turned to me.

"Hey baby boy, where ya mama at?"

"In the house beating Don."

"Ahh shit! Do I need to go save my man?"

"Nobody can save that boy," Bella said.

Focus replied, "I love you August. Make sure you stay out of her way, hear?"

"I got you Focus, and I love you more."

Bella said, "Donavin (Uncle D), watch August while I go use the bathroom, will you?"

"I got him."

I immediately noticed the rings on each of his hands.

"Uncle D, let's go to the corner store."

"August, you're with me nephew; I got you and I will let her know if she makes a scene about it."

"Make sure you do, Uncle D, because I'm two weeks clear of whippings from Thia, and I'm trying to keep it that way."

My Uncle laughed so hard it made me laugh as well. "You have my word, August. If she starts that up, I'll go to war with her on your behalf, alright?"

He put me on his shoulders then started towards the corner.

As we approached the corner store, a woman pulled her car around and parked on Milton Avenue. Uncle D put me down in the bar and told me to pick out some candy for me and Nicc while he spoke to the woman. I placed the candy on the counter and asked Uncle D if I could go out front to watch the old guy's play chess. He walked me to the door and told Tank to make sure I was good for a few minutes. Tank replied, "I got him D"

I stood on the corner for the first time, where the old guys had a table with the chess board set up against the wall. I turned to look at all the fancy cars when I noticed a suspicious looking man standing across Federal street. Another guy accompanied Tank a few feet from me on the corner. Even at seven years old, I could tell the presence of danger.

Tank was leaning on the silver light pole, while the other guy was leaning back first on the mailbox next to him. The approaching assassin's right hand was hidden inside his hoodie. As he walked across the street, his head lifted enough for me to see a white bandana covering his face from the nose down. He looked directly at me. His eyes were as cold as January. I quickly noticed a teardrop tattoo underneath his right eye. He grabbed the collar of the man leaning on the mailbox and snatched him over it. He then pulled the gun from his hoodie and put it to the guy's head.

Tank attempted to draw his gun, but his reaction was countered. The hitman turned and shot Tank in his throat before he could take aim. Everyone scattered before Tank could hit the ground. The gunman then placed the gun to the back of his intended victim's head and fired two shots before releasing him. As he turned to walk back across the street, the guy's victim slid down the mailbox with the left side of his head hanging off. He fell forward onto his face.

I felt myself being thrown onto my uncle's shoulder. He ran as fast as he could.

Chapter 3

Uncle D made a sharp left onto Rose Street and then another right up our alley towards our back door. Meanwhile, Thia ran out the front door with Bella looking for me. We heard Thia crying out for me from around the corner. I was sure that I was getting an ass whippin' on sight. Uncle D opened the gate and walked into the yard with me.

He put me down on the back porch and told me to listen to him. "If Thia asks you where you were at, tell her that you were inside of the bar with me, do you understand?"

"I got it."

As he was catching his breath, he told me to promise, and I did. He put the key in the back door and opened it.

When we got in the kitchen, Don was in the living room yelling, "Here he is!"

Bella heard Don and called for Thia to come back in the house. She was all over the hood searching for me because my Uncle had to page her. Bella was holding onto Don and I saying the Lord's Prayer while Uncle D stood watch at the front door for his sister.

Finally, Thia walked in and marched into the living room. As soon as she saw me, she just fell to her knees and pulled me in so tightly that I wished that she had whipped me instead. She was crying so hard that her tears baptized me. She eventually pulled Don in for the crucial hug as well. Focus walked in and Uncle D pulled him to the side to tell him what happened. Bella was still praying over us when Uncle D signaled for Thia to come in the basement with them. My mother gave us both a kiss and told Bella not to let us out of her sight. Bella agreed.

Both Focus and Uncle D were waiting by the basement door in the kitchen. Thia got up and told us to sit on the couch and watch TV. Then she made her way to the basement. The both of them followed her down afterwards. Later in the evening, as Bella prepared dinner for us, Thia came into the living room and sat beside me; Uncle D was standing in the dining room. She said, "Baby boy, you almost killed me today."

I gave her a confusing look.

She continued, "I should've been there to keep you safe."

"That's alright Thia; Uncle D did what you would've done."

"I'm going to ask you a question and I want the truth."

"Yes ma'am."

"If I get anything but the truth then you and everyone else in this house will be sorry, ok?"

Her approach was different this time. No cursing. Maybe she had a new technique, but she asked the inevitable question: "What happened?"

I knew that it was best for Uncle D's sake, so I replied convincingly, "I was in the bar with Uncle D and his girlfriend."

"Girlfriend?!" She turned to Uncle D and gave him a stern gaze.

Donavin answered sharply, "Alright, Althia, Damn!"

Seemingly satisfied with his answer, she rubbed me on my face and told me to go wash my hands for dinner. Before I made it up the steps, Uncle D winked his eye at me, and I did the same.

That night, we ate dinner as a family. It was a quiet dining experience for the first time ever. Don and I finished quickly to escape the painful atmosphere of dead silence. (Tank was a dear friend of Thia's. He would often run errands for her from time to time.)

We took our plates to the sink and headed upstairs. We managed to take our baths and put ourselves to bed. Thia came to check up on us a little while after. When she came into our room, she didn't speak much, but she kissed us both and just watched us. I eventually fell asleep and before I knew it, Saturday morning had arrived. When my eyes parted, my Uncle D was the first image in sight. I looked over the bunk towards Don's bed, and he wasn't there. Uncle D had this serious look on his face.

He broke the silence. "Good morning nephew."

"Wus up Uncle D. Where's everybody?"

"Everyone is downstairs; I wanted to bring you down but only after I speak to you first, ok? How are you kid?"

"I'm good Uncle D."

"Good. I want to thank you for keeping your word to me, August. I want you to just listen to me, ok? What happened yesterday was a small fraction of the world we are living in and even though you weren't meant to be there, you were. Do you like science, A?"

"Yes, I guess."

"Ok, when you're older, you'll learn about the billions of cells in your body and millions of them die every day while millions more are born. We live in a society of different mind states, and we can't say whose way is right or wrong. The nature of life is dualistic."

"What does that mean?"

"We have birth and death, hot and cold, light and dark. Everything has a counterpart, an opponent, and a challenger; do you understand?"

"Kind of."

"It's like Thia and Bella, how they can live together but don't always get along."

"I understand."

"Good! As you get older, you will grow accustomed to the saying what goes around comes around. As long as we accept that, then we can accept the consequences of our choices. Don't make the mistake I've made by leaving your family unattended!"

"I promise Uncle D."

"The name of your mission from this moment on is vigilance, understand?" He pulled a piece of small paper from his back pocket and read it to me.

"Vigilance: *alertly watchful especially to avoid danger*. Meaning as you watched the whole situation on the corner take place, I want you to always watch people, how they move, who they hang with, what they wear and how they look, ok? Stay vigilant at all times."

"So I'm-a secret agent?"

"No, you just better always pay attention, you got me?"

"Yes, I will always stay vigilant Uncle."

"Good; for the sake of your family, stay on point, nephew."

I took what he said seriously and knew what he was telling me would serve me for many years to come.

Chapter 4

My uncle picked me up and put me on his back then started down the stairs. I knew he loved me very much and I felt by keeping my mouth shut, he trusted me with just about anything at this point.

Everybody was in the kitchen. Bella was at the table with Don, while Thia was making the plates She turned and looked at me with this beautiful smile.

"Good morning baby boy."

"Hey Thia."

"How are you, my son?"

"I'm good. Just rapping to Uncle D."

"Have a seat, so you can eat."

Uncle D put me down onto the chair and sat next to me. Thia served everyone's plate before she sat down. Bella blessed the table. As she was praying, I noticed my mother was wearing the same rings as Uncle D and Focus on both of her index fingers. The Q is always on the right and the G is on the left.

As we ate, I asked about the rings. "What do your rings mean, Uncle D?"

The three of them stopped and zeroed in on me. Thia answered sharply, "Eat ya damn food boy and mind your business." Don looked at me and shook his head, signaling for me not to ask about it again.

Suddenly, the house phone rang and Thia got up to answer it. After a few moments, Thia excused herself from her call to address me. "Why didn't I tell her that Mr. Phil came by yesterday?"

Bella cut in. "Leave the boy alone, Thia! you know what happened yesterday!"

"I know what happened but if someone gives you a message for any of us, you always deliver it, no matter what

August! Don't let anything sidetrack you because the message could be important.

Thia hung up the phone and told us to finish eating so we could get dressed and go across the street to the record shop and listen to music. Don and I loved that place a lot. We finished up and went to our room.

"Don what's up with the rings on their fingers and why can't we know about them?"

Don replied, "Don't ever ask about the rings again."

I noticed Don's mood became defensive and words were extremely blunt. However, since Don's twelfth birthday, he had been more to himself and reading a lot.

We headed downstairs and into the living room. I turned on the TV while Don buried his head into his book along with his notepad. Bella was next door with Ms. Flemings. We could hear them through the front window. I decided to go and sit on the front stoop. It was the first time I'd been outside since the incident at the corner. The hood was the same as if nothing had happened and the corner was back to normal. We were so immune to death on the east side; afterwhile, it wasn't a big thing.

I looked to my left and spotted Nicci Boy dashing down the street towards me. "Wus up A!"

"Wus up Nicc?" As he walked up on the stoop and gave me a pound he said, "I heard about what happened. Did you hear about Tank and Gamo getting killed? That was the other guy's name?"

"Yeah, Gamo was the one the guy came for, I heard. Who told you Nicc?"

"My brother E -- he knew them both. They were pushing for R.J."

"Who?"

"The nigga who controls the east side boy!"

"Alright, calm down; I didn't know. He's like God to some people. Speaking of which, are you going to church with us tomorrow?"

"Hell no A, that shit is boring!"

Bella heard Nicci boy and responded, "Boy get over here!"

He walked over to her and she said, "Why are you talking like you are grown and who taught you how to talk like that?!"

"Sorry, Ms. Bella."

"Dominique, you are 7 years old. Don't ever speak like that again, especially around August, hear me?"

"Yes, Ms. Bella."

Ms. Flemings went into the house and got a piece of soap and instructed Nicci to put it in his mouth and not to swallow. Nicci just looked at me.

Ms. Flemings said to Nicci, "I want you to tell Donna what I did and why, you hear me?" Nicci nodded and she instructed him to spit it out and go home.

He ran up the street and Bella snapped at me, "You know better, don't you?!"

"Yes."

"Ok then!"

Thia came to the door asking what happened?

Bella replied, "Nothing but the devil!"

Soon Thia was ready to go to Phil's, and she invited my friends to come with us. She was beautiful in her all-white outfit. She wore a white head wrap and a white linen suit. Her rings were on display, along with her big, silver hooped earrings. She was always conservative and never revealed anything to the public.

She kissed me on my forehead, and I took her hand and walked down the steps with her as Don, E, and Nicci ran down the street towards us. Ms. Donna came to her front door and yelled, "You can have 'em Thia!" My mother laughed out loud and said, "They all mine today girl!"

Ms. Donna replied, "I know that's right."

We all huddled up and ran across the street on Thia's command. Everybody in the neighborhood was speaking to my mother -- from the dope fiends to the drug dealers up to the decent people who went to work every day. She had that kind of effect, and she knew how to handle the attention.

We got across the street, and I immediately spotted Mr. Phil standing in the front door of his store smoking a cigar with Luther Vandross playing, "The Power of Love."

As we approached the corner entrance, he spoke. "Hey fellas, wus the word?"

He held his fist out so we could all pound it in an assembly line. He hugged Thia and kissed her hand as she walked in.

There were rows of records on shelves like a library all in alphabetical order. He had pictures of old artists all over the walls in a different corner of the store. The walls were red brick with hardwood floors that shined. The windows were at the top of the store on the second level. Mr. Phil's office was on the ground level in the back of the store. There were steps that led up to the second level, which led to another room.

Don and E asked Althia could they go to the court across the street at Lakewood, and she agreed. She told Nicci and I to go and listen to music in Phil's office.

We ran into the back with Mr. Phil and settled in. After about five minutes, my uncle and Focus came into the store and walked upstairs with Thia and Phil. Thia pulled out a key and opened the door. They all went in for a few minutes before Phil and my uncle came out. Phil went downstairs, while my uncle sat in a chair by the office door.

Meanwhile, Mr. Phil was at the entrance welcoming people in. I recognized some of them from the neighborhood and others I didn't. There were about seven people. They followed Phil upstairs and sat on the couches. My uncle nodded at Mr. Phil and told the first lady to go in. She had an envelope, along with the others. Uncle D gave her a slight pat down and even looked in her purse before letting her in. As time went on, I watched as the assembly line shrunk down to the last man.

That night, Don and I ate dinner alone. Bella was at Ms. Flemings again. Everyone else was in the basement, and Don was reading at the table as we ate.

I broke the silence and asked, "What are you reading?"

"The Pale Horse," Don replied!

"What's that about?"

"Before I tell you, I want you to do something first."

"What?"

"Knowledge is the word." As he was speaking, he tore a piece of paper out of his pad and wrote the word on the piece of paper, and said to find the meaning and copy it. He slid the dictionary towards me and began to read again.

I disregarded my meal and started flipping through the dictionary to complete my search. At that very minute, Focus came through the basement door and said, "Save the books until after y'all eat. Thia will have a fit if y'all aren't finished by 9 boys." He put his right index finger on my sheet of paper and said, "Knowledge is understanding gained by actual experience or a clear perception of truth."

Don leaned back in his chair as if Focus had spoiled his appetite. Focus said, "Give me the pen; this one is on the house baby boy."

He wrote it down and told me to study the definition.

He gave Don a pound and walked towards the front door as Uncle D came up the steps. He put both hands on our shoulders and wished us a goodnight. I immediately heard Focus' engine ignite, and they were off. When I turned, I saw Thia standing at the basement door. She told us to hurry up and get ready for church tomorrow. She went upstairs to run my bath water.

Don asked me if I understood what Focus told me about the word. "Yeah, knowledge is gained by personal experience, right?" The paper was still in front of me, of course. He nodded and we both finished our meal and cleaned up.

I started up the steps and went straight into the bathroom. After my bath, I got myself ready for bed as Don went to take his shower. As I laid on the top bunk watching the ceiling, Thia came into the room and stood at the side of my bed for a brief moment.

As she walked away, I asked, "Thia what were y'all doing at Mr. Phil's store?"

"Goodnight August," she said in a soft voice. She then cracked the door and turned the light off in one motion.

Don came into the room a while after and got ready for bed himself.

After Don got settled in, he read for a while before going to sleep. I followed soon after. Before I knew it, Bella was in our room waking us up for church.

Chapter 5

"C'mon boys, it's time for worship; the van will be here within the hour. Get up and get dressed," Bella commanded.

Bella was definitely in her mode this morning. We got to the kitchen table and found breakfast waiting for us. Focus was sitting in the living room with Uncle D speaking in low tones as usual. Thia kissed us both and said good morning to us.

As Don and I started on the plates, Thia signaled for D and Focus to come down into the basement. Shortly after, Bella came downstairs. She sat at the dining room table in a *humming mood.* Bella had a beautiful voice, and she would sing every Sunday. The church van pulled up and honked for us. Thia shot up the steps to see us off. She walked us out and into the van and gave us both 5 dollars to put into the collection plate. She helped Bella onto the van before she started back into the house. Don went to sleep as soon as he got comfortable. The driver, Mr. Kevin, asked Bella about the incident that occurred on Friday, and she quickly evaded the conversation.

Our family was very tight with info, especially when it involved anyone from within. I was watching, as we ventured through the East side. We made our way through Highlandtown, Orleans Street, Monument Street, Harford Road, and finally Belair Road before we headed west into the Sandtown area. From the looks of it, West Baltimore was all the same. Pennsylvania Avenue was like Monument Street -- packed with so many people who were selling everything.

Finally, we made our way back to the east side of Greenmount Avenue. We all headed inside knowing that we had a long day ahead of us.

I couldn't help but to think about the murder that took place in front of me. I'd thought nothing of it until I got here in a place where Jesus is said to always protect us from all things evil. Reality had won me over and at 7 years old, I knew that a person could walk up to you and do anything they wanted to do and nothing was coming out of the sky to stop them. As the service went on, I rushed to the bathroom and threw up in the toilet. It took me a few minutes to regain myself before I heard a knock on the door. It was Bella.

"August, what's wrong?"

"I feel sick."

"Did you throw up?"

"Yes ma'am but, I'm better now." She brought me into the church's kitchen and sat me on her lap.

"Was it the breakfast or have you been feeling sick and not telling anyone?"

At that point I wanted to tell her about the murder, but I had promised Uncle D to never speak on it so for the first time I lied to Bella.

"No Bella, my stomach just didn't feel good but, I'm better now".

She put my head on her heart and just cradled me until the end of the day.

When we got home, the house was spotless. Everyone was in the backyard conversing. Don announced us as we came in, and Thia came thru the back screen door to greet us with kisses.

"Hey boys, how was church?"

We replied in unison: "Fine!"

Bella spoke up, "August was sick today but he got it together, didn't you?"

"Um hmm."

Thia put her hands on my face. "What happened baby boy?"

"Nothing… my stomach was hurting."

"OK, are you in the mood for pizza?'

"Yes," both Don and I replied. She reached for the oven and pulled out a homemade sausage and cheese pizza. We sat down and went to work on it while Thia went back outside. Bella went upstairs. She was tired after church. She said goodnight and we said the same.

I then asked Don, "How do you feel about God?"

He looked at me and said, "God is everywhere and *never* question that, you hear me?!"

"Yeah, yeah, so why is everything so fucked up then Don? People getting their brains blown out and life doesn't stop. People don't care at all. Why God doesn't stop that from happening Don?"

"August shut the fuck up; you ain't seen shit for real boy!"

"I've seen more than your fake Jordan ass."

"Boy, I'm the shit on that black top and you know that."

"Don, you haven't noticed how the city is with the drugs?"

Don laughed uncontrollably. "Don't worry about it boy; just be a kid August."

"I'm-a tell Uncle D to beat all the drug dealers up for me."

"A, just take your time and understand how the world works before you make decisions on how to change it.

Believe it or not, your family feels the same way, so leave it at that August."

Don got up from the table and went upstairs. Little did I know, Uncle D was standing at the back screen door listening to us the entire time.

Chapter 6

The next morning, I was up around 6 am getting ready for school. Education and behavior were very big things in my house.

I grabbed my bookbag and headed for the door. Thia was already at work, so Don took me to school. He went to the middle school around the corner with Nicci's brother, E. I found myself on the front stoop watching all the kids walking to school with their older siblings as well.

Uncle D came to the door.

"Good morning August, time to take it back to school huh?"

"Yeah, it looks that way." Uncle D laughed and said, "I will be picking you up today, ok, and we will go hang out. I already told Thia."

"Ard then Uncle," then he added, "So look for me in the school yard."

School started at 7:30, but I liked to hang in the school yard with my buddy before then. As we passed Nicci's house, I heard shouting inside the house. For some reason, I knew something was wrong. We made our way across the busy street and Mr. Phil was standing in the doorway of his shop sharp as usual.

"What it is boys?"

"Ain't too much," Don replied. "Y'all play it cool today, hear?"

"We got you, Mr. Phil."

Don gave me a pound and told me to represent the family. Don and I loved each other though we rarely admitted it. He turned around and walked off. I went into the yard into an ocean of kids. I searched for Nicci, only to find him leaning up against the fence in the far corner. I walked towards him with haste.

"Wus hood Nicc?" He picked his head up.

"Wassup yo?"

I noticed tears in his eyes. I leaned on the fence next to him and asked him what was wrong.

He wiped his eyes and asked, "You're my man, right A?"

"You already know Nicc, why?"

"Let's go down Patterson Park and watch the games on the court. Fuck school, it will be here."

"Ard, but my Uncle is picking me back up after school so I gotta be back here."

"I got you A."

We made our way through the crowd back on to Luzerne Street. Mr. Phil's store was directly across the street, but he went inside so we were all clear. Eventually, we stopped at the corner store on Milton Ave and Hoffman to grab snacks before we started to the court. We both knew our way to the park, thanks to Don and E. They spent all of their time there and sometimes took us along, so we knew where to find them. As we were walking, Nicci boy seemed intrigued by the local drug gangs setting up their shops.

Nicc interrupted my thoughts. "August, life is about a dollar and I-ma do whatever I have to do to get it. My father was a kingpin, and he went to the feds for taking care of us. I talked to him this morning before school, and he told me that he will be home in 5 years and things will be better. I promised him that I would help to support the family."

He was so ambitious for a 7-year-old, but we both were and that's why we were so tight. However, we didn't share the same interests at all. I never admired the bosses, but I would be lying if I said I didn't want the power that they had. However, they never lasted --either falling to the feds, their own product, or the "museum," which is what we called the graveyard.

I always had the foresight to see the bigger picture, but Nicci didn't give a fuck. His choice was already made. Hooking school was a first for me, but I felt he had to tell me something and loyalty was my weakness as I would find out later. The deeper we got into the eastside the more depressing it got. Needles in the gutter, a strung-out mother standing in dope lines with her children at her side. All the while, Nicc was fascinated with the opportunity of making some real money. He was taken by the images and after hearing his plans with his father, why wouldn't he be? We arrived at the courts on Baltimore Street and it was live. All the middle school and high school dope boys were there placing bets as usual. Nicc and I blended in with the crowd. If Thia found out, it was over for me. They were announcing the players on the mic by their hoods and nicknames. Believe it or not, there were a few females out there as well. They announced that the game would start in 15 minutes. The walk there alone was time consuming, and I had no idea it was that late. To no surprise, I saw Don in full gear. I had seen him play before and he had his game face on as focus had a camcorder trained onto him. This shit was getting deep and if I didn't stay hidden, I would drown for sure. The game was about to start and both teams were doing layups and jumpers.

I tore open my pack of penny candies that Nicci boy paid for with his lunch money. They lined up for the jump ball and I could see the money being exchanged from the side bets between the drug gang representatives. Ten minutes in, Don was in full Jordan mode. Shooting people's lights out, finger rolling and all kinds of shit. The competition was intense on both ends due to "baby John" being on the opposite team. He was the truth too! 6'1, light skinned and slim. He was a dunker. He was also Big John Zelmore's son. Big John was a cocaine boss in the Highlandtown area. He was there as well to support his son. The females were doing their part to the utmost making their mark on the court. Before we knew it, halftime had arrived. I watched Don as he went to the bench but I had lost track of Focus.

As I scanned the crowd for him, I felt a big hand grab the back of my neck and force me to turn around. It was him of course. Nicci was assaulted as well. He marched us both out of the court and threw us up against the fence.

"You two look just like some little boys I know and it can't be them because, 2nd grade would be that way." He punched both of us in the stomach making us collapse to the grass.

While we were gasping for air and drooling he spoke.

"I've seen a lot of shit in my years but, never have I witnessed two babies hooking school. Y'all aren't even able to protect yourselves and I'm family, so imagine what a stranger could do to you? Both of you stand on ya feet."

We summoned our strength to stand before he gave us further instructions. "Place your back up against the fence! Before I take you back to school we will have class right here first, so raise your hands if you have a question. Class starts in a minute so please take your seats."

He pushed downward on our shoulders to put us in the squat position before he walked back into the court to check on Don. After a little while our legs were on the fire and Nicci was folding. Tears started to pour out of his eyes and he was calling Focus all kinds of bitches and punks, but he knew not to get his ass off that fence.

Focus finally returned with two water bottles and said, "Today's lesson is about pressure and how well you can function under it. Do you know what pressure is, fellas?" We both shook our heads no.

"Ok. Pressure is the burden of physical or mental distress. For example, "When I punched you two in the stomach, I applied pressure which made you fall to the ground, you got it?!"

I replied, "Yes sir."

"Oh, so now I'm sir. Do you see what pressure does to people? What's two plus two?"

Nicci raised his hand, "Four!"

"Good, nine plus three?"

Nicci beat me to it again, "Twelve!

"Good, one plus four?"

I raised my hand, "Five!"

"Good. What is pressure?"

I answered, "Mental and physical distress!"

"Great! Final question. What do y'all want to be when you're older?"

I answered, "Vigilant!" Focus smiled and nodded with approval. "Now you Nicc?"

"I want to be a kingpin!"

I watched Focus as he exploded. "What the fuck are you talking about Dominique?!"

"It's in my blood and I don't need no weak-ass school to show me how to get paid!"

"How will you manage your money then Nicci!"

"I will pay someone to do it for me."

"So you want to profit from the downfall of your own people?"

"Fuck them people and fuck this shit!" Nicci boy tried to walk but his legs were too weak, and he fell forward in pain.

Focus stood over top of Nicci and softly said, "Pressure bursts pipes." Then he turned his attention to me and said, "But, it also makes diamonds."

As he picked Nicci up, he told me to stand. He told us both to take a knee and catch our breath while handing us the bottles of water. It was about 80 degrees outside so the water did us some justice after that whole ordeal. While we were taking a knee, I couldn't help but notice Big John coming out of the court with his two security homeboys at each side. He had a cigar hanging from his mouth. His bodyguards were known as the "Mac Twins." I knew that much. Focus was locked in on him as well with a sharp gaze and a sinister smirk. Both of his rings shined in the sunlight as he massaged them both with his thumbs.

He looked at Nicc and said, "Go get his autograph!"

Nicc sucked his teeth and stood up. "Man, can I go to school?"

"That's the smartest shit you said all day boy. Let's move you two!"

We approached the Chevelle at the end of the trail and got in the backseat. In no time, we were back at the school. Focus whipped out a pad and wrote us doctor's notes to pardon our tardiness. We got out of the car, walked to the entrance, and rang the bell. While we waited to get buzzed in, Focus warned us, "Try this again, and I will be more creative with your consequence. Education should be your first priority and if you want to make it in this world, drug dealer or not, you must master this first. Learn what they have to teach you and then some before you make a final decision."

The door buzzed and we went directly to the office. We came in and sat on the bench while focus went to the desk and covered for us. Nicci and I were quiet until Focus told us to go to class. I gave him a pound and Nicc kept it moving.

As I was walking down the hall, Focus called me one last time and asked me which one are you -- the Pipe or the Diamond?

"I'm the diamond," I responded.

"Good, so that means pressure is your friend. Next time you're faced with a decision that you know isn't righteous and the pressure is on, what do you do?"

"I will be the diamond."

"I hear you; go on I'll see you later."

I ran off to class knowing he wouldn't say a word to Thia and that was good enough not to try it again. I walked into the classroom and gave my teacher the note before taking a seat next to Nicc. Soon after, we were lining up for lunch and heading to the cafeteria. We sat together and as usual, Nicc was aggravated. I figured it was motivated by us being caught up by Focus, but it was something more with him. He was quiet for the rest of the day and before you knew it, school was over.

Chapter 7

Finally, the bell sounded, and we were off towards the school yard. I asked Nicc if he was coming outside and that's when he broke it to me.

"August, I'm going to stay with my uncle in Cherry Hill and this was my last day. My mother told my father that I was too much, so I need a man in my life. Her and my father have been talking about it for a few months." That's why he wanted me to skip school with him because it was our last ride together for a while. He said that he would visit in the summer.

We were standing in the school yard for a while letting the other kids fan out when my uncle appeared at the steps. It slipped my mind that he was coming. He signaled for us to come towards him.

While walking toward Uncle D, I quickly asked, "Is that why you were crying this morning?"

He nodded in return.

Uncle D walked us across the street and told me to put my backpack in the car. Ms. Donna was standing in her doorway as fine as she wanted to be with a suitcase on the front steps.

"Hey August, how was school?"

"Fine Ms. Donna."

"Did Nicci tell you he was leaving today?"

"Yes ma'am."

Uncle D turned to me and insisted that I speak to my buddy for a few before we left.

Nicci and I sat on his front stoop one last time. We finished our candy and I told Nicc what I had seen that last Friday on the corner. Nicci was shocked!

"Did you see Tank get killed too?"

"Yeah, and the guy who did it had a teardrop on his face."

"Damn A, even I ain't never seen nobody get smoked before. Do you have dreams about it?"

"No, but I won't forget it."

Nicc put his arm around me and said, "August, that's the world we live in my nigga, that's why we gotta always stick together no matter what."

Suddenly, I saw a white Ford Expedition pull up in front of us. The guy got out and began walking towards us until he got to the stoop.

"Nicci boy. I'm your uncle Nod, do you remember me?"

"Not really."

Nod put his hand out for Nicci to shake it and he did. He then turned his attention to me with the same gesture. Before I could shake his hand, Uncle D told me it was time to leave. Uncle D made it up the street with haste, put his hand on my head and guided me off the steps.

Nod and Uncle D locked eyes for a minute until Ms. Donna broke the silence and introduced the two of them to each other. They both nodded. Uncle D gave Nicci a pound and told him to be good and to come back and see us soon.

"You got it," Nicci said.

Uncle D and I walked to the car, and I climbed into the backseat. Focus was sitting on the front stoop and Don was bouncing the ball in front of the house as usual. Uncle D got in the driver's seat and told Focus he would be back.

"Take ya time!" Focus replied.

Nicci boy ran to the car and knocked on the backseat window. I rolled it down and he gave me a pound and said, "August, hold the block down for me."

I gave him a pound back and said, "You got it Nicci boy; See you later."

We pulled off and Nicci threw up the peace sign up and I did the same. As we drove further down Federal Street, the image of my buddy faded more and more. I turned to Uncle D as he drove with his right arm across the head of the front seat and his left hand on the wheel. His ring beamed in the light from the windshield. As we passed the local drug havens, he asked me what did I see.

I answered, "Pipes."

"What pipes are you talking about?"

"I see what pressure does to pipes and what it makes people do."

We stopped at a red light, and he looked back in shock for a minute. "Do you know about pressure?"

"I know it's physical and mental stress. Many people fold like lawn chairs while others become diamonds." Then I informed him that the light had turned green. He turned to continue driving.

"I see you're more vigilant than I thought. Nephew, never think that drugs are the way and don't get hooked up in the allure of the material things they acquire. Always remember that time is the real judge. Longevity is in your blood and lineage. Always choose family overall and that includes close friends. In some cases, blood makes you related but loyalty makes you family, understand?"

"I got it uncle, family right?"

"Yeah, honor lies in your deeds especially when you do for others."

As he spoke, I soaked it up and he knew I would. It was like Nicci and I were starting new lives that day. Little did we know that would be the last time I would see him. He never came back, but I did hold it down just as I promised my ace!

Chapter 8

Five years had passed since Nicci left, and I was like a prince in the hood as my family's influence grew. I was twelve years old in the winter of '99 and well into the seventh grade at Hamilton Middle School on the north side of town. Don had just turned seventeen in November and he was working closely with Thia at Mr. Phil's. He was her driver after he got his license, plus he was graduating that year. As a result, Thia gave him more freedom to do what he liked.

His girlfriend, Neka, was always over the house. Neka was heavy set, brown-skinned, about 5'6, and had a pretty smile. We all loved her as if she was family so she fit straight in with us. Bella still did church faithfully and dragged us along every Sunday. Thia was like a goddess on the East Side. Everyone wanted to be next to her. Most women wanted to *be her*. Focus and Uncle D were her bodyguards, and they were still undisputed as far as I was concerned. We were more fortunate in every way. We had better furniture, glass tables, imported rugs, etc. Ray redid our kitchen and bathroom for us. We even had a new front and back door with black heavy screen doors to match. Uncle D had a black Lincoln Town car with white walls on the tires. Thia had a white STS Cadillac coupe that Don usually drove all the time.

While we were thriving, the neighborhood was under turmoil due to the death of 5 bosses and other major players over the years. The infamous cocaine Boss K.J. was gone to the Feds and left a big void in the game that everyone wanted to fill. The only bosses left were Big John, Prince Riley, and some old-timer named Demetri who just came home. It was a few days after the new year, and the murder rate was sky-high. Now known as the bloody 90s, unfortunately, it was the era I grew up in. The wars ignited after a few of the bosses were assassinated a couple of years back. No one knew who killed any of them so the drug gangs went to war with each other over territory.

The older I got, the more things I noticed about my family and what they didn't take part in. For instance, holidays went uncelebrated in my house. Anybody would've mistaken us for Muslims or some shit but, it was even deeper than that.

I was given an assignment on my birthday to do a book report on the "Pale Horse," which was the same book Don had five years back. Focus told me I had one month to complete it but I finished it by mid-December.

As I reflected on the message within the book, I developed a level of vigilance that made me question every aspect of life. Everything was under scrutiny from religion to politics.

Bella moved over to West Baltimore with her brother a year back, so I took her room. She did it so I could have my own space.

It was a Tuesday night, and I was in my room finishing my report at my desk. Wasn't sure what time it was but it had to be late because the house was quiet. There was a silhouette on the floor from the light in the hallway.

"Who goes there?" I stated without looking.

Focus responded, "What are you up to?"

"Just getting this report done."

"Didn't I tell you to bring me the book when you finished reading it?"

"Yeah, but I had to write the report."

"The purpose is to remember what you've read." He walked over and grabbed my report then tore it up. I was in total shock because it was 9 pages back and front.

All I could say was, "That's crazy Focus."

"What good is your memory if you don't use it? Now, I appreciate your efforts towards this task but your mind is fresh enough to retain information. Remember what I told you about pressure and the kind of control it has if you allow it? That lesson was physical, this one is mental August."

"I got it."

"Good, meet me in the backyard in one minute, and come as you are."

He started towards the stairs before I could let him know that all I had on was a T-shirt, some basketball shorts, and slippers. It was about 28 degrees outside. I looked out my back window and saw focus taking his position. He was standing in the backyard wearing nothing more than a sweatsuit as he stared up at me. He smiled at me, and I could see his breath leaving his body confirming that it was freezing. He then pointed to his wristwatch and I jetted down the stairs and shot through the back door.

As soon as the cold air hit me, I gasped like I had just fallen through a sheet of ice. Focus was standing at the end of the yard at the tall wooden gate that Ray also added to seclude the yard. He had his arms folded with a stern look on his face. "Welcome, and you're three seconds late. Don't worry about it though. I will get my 3 seconds back at a time you need it the most, alright."

"Yeah, Focus I got it."

"Step out here with me and let the moon be your witness, August."

As I stepped off the back porch, I scanned the yard. We had weight benches along the left side of the yard with

Olympic weights racked up on the porch. We also had a pull and dip par on the porch. Uncle D and Focus were in perfect shape, working out daily, while Thia managed their diets well. I was a foot from Focus before he reached his arm out towards me and said, "Arm's length."

I walked towards him until my forehead met his fingertips.

"Good August, now I know you hate the cold, but this is something that you will have to overcome sooner or later."

It was so cold, I could barely talk, so I just nodded. The frigid air felt like needles on my toes and fingertips. It was completely dark besides the light from the full moon shining on us.

"Let your body be all the protection you need, August. Let the light guide you even in the darkest places and in your darkest hour."

I focused on the full moon as the wind gusts penetrated my bones.

"All you know must go into exile as of now, August. What if I told you that everything you've been told for the better part of your life was a lie?"

"What do you mean?"

"Life as we know it is based on five principles set in motion to keep you in the dark ages."

"What principles Focus?"

"Entertainment, media, politics, economics, and religion are all tools of mass control of the people."

"So what I read was true?"

"Yes, but let time be your guide to see yourself. The only thing real is your family. We are as real as the winter you're standing in and if you allow us to advise you then you will expect a cunning life under the moon.

I was speechless and I felt the brisk air filling my lungs with every breath. Focus' eyes were locked dead on to mine as he waited for me to respond.

Finally, I said; "Focus, I don't know what that means as far as the moon or my family. What does it have to do with anything?"

"You are of age now to join your family in its cause and take your place among the ranks of your blood. Do you trust your family?"

"Yes."

"Then take three days to decide what truly matters in your life and where you would be without your family. Where you want to go in life and how you want to get there.

Suddenly I felt a blanket thrown over my shoulders. I turned to find Thia at my rescue instructing me to go to bed. I made my way into the house with haste. Don and Uncle D were at the kitchen table conversing in a soft tone. They didn't even notice me passing by, so I just kept it moving all the way to my room. As soon as I got to my room, I immediately buried myself under my bed sheets.

I could still feel the frigid air in my lungs as I drew in deep breaths. When I took my head from under the blanket, I saw Thia standing over me with her arms at parade rest behind her back.

She broke the silence. "My son, I brought you some hot chocolate with marshmallows." She then nodded towards the mug on my desk. I immediately peeled the blankets off and headed straight for the cup. As I took my first sip, I sat on the edge of my bed as Thia sat in the chair at my desk facing me. She never broke her stare, and I could tell from her demeanor that this conversation would be different from all the others.

She leaned back into the chair and crossed her legs. "August, you're my baby boy and I have high hopes for you."

Before I could answer, she waved her hand and said, "Just listen to me. This family is very important to this neighborhood and our cause is valuable to this city because of our successful resistance to tyranny. Over the past few years, you've witnessed the power and influence we've obtained on the eastside. This is because the people believe in us, for we have given them something to believe in regardless of the harsh realities we come from. As you know, Don is going away to Penn State next year, and I will need you to step up in his place and help me out with a few things."

As she spoke to me, her rings were on display as her hands were on her knees while her legs were crossed.

"Do you have any questions, August?"

"Yeah, what do you do over at Mr. Phil's in the office?"

"Well, I consider managing dire circumstances that prove too dangerous for the average person."

"Why do they come to you?"

"I just told you August!"

"Yeah, but why come to you of all people, and what is a dire circumstance?"

"A dire circumstance is a horrible or dreadful situation, like a warning of disaster. People come to me because I'm capable and I have the means to do so, baby boy."

Thia grabbed me by my face and kissed my forehead then made her way towards the door. "Get some rest, you have school in the morning."

The door shut behind her engulfing me in darkness once again. I finished my cup and sat it on the desk. I took a few minutes to think about all Thia had said. At that moment, I knew that my family was extremely weird in more ways than one but their sincerity intrigued me in a way that made me feel obligated to join them. I was beginning to understand why I was so loved in the neighborhood. My mother made it clear why we were so relevant in the slums. Truthfully, I hated to be left out when my folks would go into the basement or meet up at Mr. Phil's. They never talked around me and when they did, I could sense that their words were censored. Don was the same age when he started to change and conform to certain activities around the house. Over time, I watched Don become reliable and more respectful towards others as well as his own family. He was also at the height of his game but ironically, he wasn't going to Penn State because he could ball. He got a scholarship for his academic achievements. That's what made me respect him most of all and somehow, I know the family had a lot to do with his success.

Chapter 9

My alarm clock went off at 6 am. I took a shower and got dressed. I headed downstairs and into the kitchen and made myself some breakfast. Class started at 8:30, but I always made a small detour beforehand.

I finished my breakfast and went to stand on my front stoop to wait for the bus when I spotted some kids from the neighborhood walking to school in packs. I automatically thought about my long-lost homie. Ms. Donna had moved out of the hood two years prior. While I was reminiscing, I noticed a white car with gold trim easing its way down Federal Street slowly past my house. I couldn't see through the tinted windows, but I never broke eye contact as it kept easing down the street until it was out of sight. I glanced to my left and saw the bus making its way, so I locked the door and ran to the corner. The bus pulled up. I got on, flashed my pass, and strolled towards the back. It was about 27 degrees outside, so I made sure that I sat under the heating vent next to the window. Since I went to school out of zone, my commute was always a tour through the city.

There were so many vacant houses on every street. It made me question the lack of progress our community was truly making and whether or not the influence of my family could reach beyond Federal Street. I was no saint though and thanks to Don, and his homie, Man I got drafted to the weed team. Rolling my blunts on the back of the bus became the norm but smoking with Jenell every morning was a ritual. Now I don't want to stereotype Jamaicans, but this bitch was a full-blown pothead at twelve years old. I got off the bus at Monument Street and jumped on another for about 5 minutes later. The further I went North, the better the view got. It was a different world up here and at that moment I realized why Thia wanted me to go to school up here rather than East Baltimore. The environment had more opportunities and less distractions. Her decision made me upset at first but the older I got, things made more sense on a larger scale.

I got off at the library on old Hartford Road. My school was on the same street but I cut a corner towards

Jenell's house. Her folks were middle class for the most part and they stayed in a four-bedroom house. Jenell stayed with both of her parents and three younger siblings. Her room was in the basement, so I never had to knock because she left the side door open for me every morning. I always took the alley because of her neighbors. I jumped her fence, walked towards the side door, and went in.

Jenell was in her boy shorts and a training bra ironing her clothes using her bed. She cut her eyes at me and smiled.

I peeled my jacket and hoodie off over my head and tossed them both onto her couch. I made my way over to her wrapped my hands around her from the back and kissed her neck. Afterward, I pulled the blunt out of my jacket and asked, "How much time do we have Nell?"

"Five minutes until eight. We're good for a 'wake n bake'."

I laughed and lit the blunt with her lighter that was on the coffee table. She came over and climbed onto my lap to join me. Janell had jet-black skin and thick black hair.

I could tell Nell had seen some things in her life. The Jamaican flag was on display over her bed with the black number 13 stitched in the center. That was her hood in Kingston, where some are called "Rats." We finished up and headed out at about 8:15.

We made it to school on time and made our way to her locker.

"Seriously Nell, let's build something we can stand on. I'm more than ready, and I feel you are too; just think about it." I gave her a kiss and made my way to class.

The highlight of my day was pretty much my 3rd period language arts class. Due to the intense book reports my family had me engaged in at a young age, it made me a very good reader and comprehensive beyond my years. I was one of those kids who had no problem reading aloud; in fact, I often volunteered to do so. Miss Larue, or Miss L for short, taught my favorite subject. A light skinned, green eyed vixen who just happened to be a teacher rather than a model. Her toes were always out and done. I remember being in church on Sunday with Bella praying for Miss L to be a sex offender.

Participating was not a problem, and I became one of her favorites. However, the situation with Focus was still on my mind as well as the conversation with Thia. I still had two days to decide my role in the family. School was a way to leave the pressure and be amongst the mere mortals.

My peers had no clue about my status in the hood. Even though I didn't have to work for it myself, it was as real as if I did. Truth be told, I knew very little about what it took to build the family, but I knew education was the key. My folks always told me to learn the ways of this country, the government, and its infrastructure. So all in all, Don and I received two types of education: The books we were given at home blew the whistle on the broken system of the United States. We were taught to learn all they had to teach in school and sort through the bullshit as we went along.

Don was a math wiz and I was the reader. Whatever area we lacked, we helped each other out. As we made our way out of the room, Ms. L signaled for me to approach her desk.

She started by saying, "August Joyner, one of my favorite pupils. I've noticed your level of attention towards my assignments is on point and I'm happy with the effort you put towards participating in class. At this point, you're reading at a tenth-grade level. Tell me August, what is your passion as far as language arts goes?"

"Truthfully, Ms. L, I don't like not knowing things or how they work. Plus, I don't want to be counted among the weak or dumb."

She smiled and said, "You are something, and at this rate, you will be something more in the future. Is there anything I can get you to occupy your leisure time at home, any topic at all?"

"I'd like to know more about the symbols our government uses in our society and some of the ancient societies before us."

"Wow, that's interesting; maybe I will look into it as well. I will have something for you after school, just stop by and pick it up."

"Ok. You got it."

I headed to math class. A half hour in, I saw Nell in the hallway signaling for me. I grabbed the hall pass from my teacher's desk and excused myself. We would always meet up on the stairway for a minute or two. She pulled me in the corner and kissed me with passion. As vigilant as I thought I was, the next confrontation blindsided me. We heard a loud snap then a stern voice.

"Separate!"

We both immediately did so and focused our attention to the bottom of the stairs. It was Ms. Larue shaking her head with her left hand on her hip and the other cuffing what I assumed to be my assignment. We were paralyzed with fear until Ms. L broke the silence.

"The last time I checked, this was a learning institution. The two of you are smarter than this! Please go to class, children!"

I opened the door for Nell and she jetted down the hall. I scurried behind her. I was dreading the after-school encounter with Ms. L. I knew she wouldn't report us because it would've already happened, plus getting caught was punishment enough.

After school, I met up with Nell at her locker and told her to go ahead home and that I would call her later.

Chapter 10

I made it to Ms. L's classroom and walked in. She looked up from her desk and sized me up before instructing me to have a seat. She walked from around her desk and pulled a chair up to mine. Ms. L gently placed my papers on the desk in front of me. Her fingers were interlocked and her chin was resting on them while she stared at me for a few seconds.

"These are your papers, August, concerning The great seal and certain symbols affiliated with it and our dollar bill. Now is this a good start for you Mr. Joyner?"

"Yes, Ms. L, thank you."

"Why are you so interested in this stuff anyway?"

"Well, it would be nice to find out the concept of what everyone in the city is dying for."

"I see; where are you from, August?"

"Federal street."

"Where is that exactly?"

"East Baltimore."

"So you're not from this region but you go to school here?"

"It was my mother's decision and I'm grateful."

"How are you getting home?"

"The bus."

"Well you better get to it then."

I remember leaving surprised that she didn't bring up the bullshit. After a few minutes on the bus stop, a black Acura pulled up in front of me. The passenger window slid down and Ms. Larue was gripping the wheel and signaling for me to get in. I didn't hesitate. Before I got in, I scanned my surroundings to see if anybody saw me, and I couldn't help but spot that same white Legend that rode past my house that morning. It was sitting in the convenience store parking lot across the street facing us. Focus taught me to never believe in coincidence.

I got in the car and we took off. To get a better look at the suspicious car, I placed my books into the backseat just to see if it followed us.

Ms. L broke the silence: "A simple thank you would suffice August."

"I apologize, thank you, Ms. L."

"No problem. Usually I don't give students a ride, but I couldn't help but notice you were still out here."

"Thanks again, I just missed my bus."

"If it wasn't for me holding you up, you would've caught it."

"That's true too."

She laughed a bit. My thoughts ran wild as she felt me watching her. "What, boy?!"

"How old are you Ms. L?"

"Stay in your lane, August!"

I glanced into the side mirror and the car wasn't in sight, which put me at ease, however, they still knew where I lived.

She asked, "Which is the best way to take?"

"Straight down Hartford Road then detour to Asquith Street, then make a left."

Once we passed North Avenue, the atmosphere changed and she knew it. The big houses disappeared and the infamous vacant row homes stood like monuments in an active war zone. We approached Torino's on Federal Street and made a left.

She turned the radio down and asked, "Do you live down here?"

"Yes I do and it's not so bad when you are from here Ms. L."

As we stopped at a red light, she noticed the cartels broadcasting their scrambled dope on the corner like it was legal.

"We are a long way from Hamilton, aren't we Ms. L?"

"August, you have to get away from this baby." The light turned green, and she accelerated deeper into the slums. We got to Milton Ave, and I saw Uncle D sitting on the stoop. I told her to make a right on Luzerne and park by Mr. Phil's.

Once we stopped, she started, "Where is your house?"

"I'm good here Ms. L."

As I opened the door she said, "Wait!" I locked eyes with her hoping she wanted a kiss.

"I want to hear about those papers very soon, ok?"

I nodded, then jumped out and went inside Phil's to find a line of people waiting to see my mother once again. I spoke to everyone I knew, but there were even more unfamiliar faces I didn't know. Mr. Phil was in his office with his feet on top of his desk. I made my way up the stairs and glanced through the blinds to see Don and Focus in the office with Thia. She gestured for me to enter, and I walked in immediately.

Focus shut the door behind me and said, "Wus up Prince?"

"Nothing much, Focus."

Don gave me a pound and I noticed a green record book in his other hand. The same one the teachers use in school. Thia came from around the desk and wrapped me up in her arms. "Hey, baby boy. How was school, huh?"

"It was cool as always."

"Good. Now go and sit in that booth in the far corner and wait for me to finish up here."

I left the office and walked to the last booth in the far corner of the balcony. I had a clear view into the office, and I watched as Focus let the first of many people in. Shortly after, he shut the blinds. I took off my layers of clothes and started on my homework. Math was a subject that Don did with me every night, so I saved it for later.

I finally got to my assignment that Ms. L printed out for me earlier. When I glanced up, the line was almost finished, and Uncle D was headed toward me with a large plate.

"August, wassup nephew? I brought you something to eat."

"Good looking out Uncle." I peeled the foil off and dug in. My uncle took a seat.

"What's on your mind, little Prince?"

"I have this new information I'm interested in to follow up on the book."

"Like what?"

I passed him the papers and I began to eat. My uncle asked, "Where did you get this from, the library?"

"No, I have an inside connection."

"Does it have anything to do with that "little red thang" that dropped you off earlier?" I locked eyes with him.

"Oh, you didn't think I caught that, did you? We always keep our eyes on the family, especially the Prince."

"She's my teacher, Ms. Larue, and that's my future piece, Uncle D."

He shook his head and said, "Take your time and stay young, you understand me?"

"I hear you, Uncle D. So that was you today in the white Legend?"

"What are you talking about?"

"There was a white car with gold trim following me today; isn't that how you saw me with Ms. Laure?"

"No, I saw you in the passenger's seat when y'all rode past the house. Now are you sure about this car?"

"Yeah, I saw it ride passed the house this morning before I left, and then again by my school."

"Alright, we will investigate it ASAP but for now, let's get on this subject."

He pointed his finger toward my papers and said she got this from the author Anthony T Browder. He pulled out a dollar bill and placed it flat on the table. (Uncle D explained the symbolism behind the American Currency.) "This is the nucleus of all tyranny and mankind has been at its mercy from the beginning. The barter system is the way of the world, August. At this moment, understand that everything is up for trade and you're only as good as what you can produce.

"The obverse bears the design used on official documents. The American eagle, with an escutcheon, or shield on its breast symbolizes self-reliance." An olive branch of 13 leaves and 13 olives in its right talon and 13 arrows in its left. Notice that the eagle is facing the olive branch which symbolizes a desire for peace, but it is always prepared for war. In its beak is a scroll inscribed E pluribus unum, which translates as a nation out of many states. Above the eagle's head is the 13-star "new constellation" of the 1777 flag, enclosed in a glory or golden radiance, breaking through a cloud.

"Do you understand what we are reading so far, nephew?"

"Yeah, but it will take me some time to remember all this."

"That's why you have your notes to refer back to when you need them. Never devote your mind, body, and soul to anything that you don't understand."

"So cross reference means to look up right?"

"Yeah, always try and find the source, Prince. Everything in this world is conceptualized by mankind, meaning all things had a name given to them by man. "Men even made up names for the deity they all worshiped."

"That's crazy Uncle D!"

"No it isn't; men want to be revered so they discover things, August."

"So what will you be revered for Uncle?"

"Relax Prince, let time be your guide. Wisdom takes years to obtain, but a lifetime to apply." He pointed to my temple and said, "Your bloodline is the brotherhood of redemption, and we protect our nation with a higher level of consciousness." You're at the age now where you must cast ignorance into exile!"

Focus called my Uncle once all the people were gone. I didn't notice that the place was just about empty. Uncle D got up to see what he wanted. As he walked off, I held onto his words. He broke my assignment down with detail and made me realize that these so-called wars and treachery in the street were fueled by this small piece of history.

I bet half of these so-called Bosses couldn't tell you what this meant, but they could tell you how to spend it. Another thing that got me was how my Uncle could tell what book it was from. I had never seen him read anything before. I finished my meal and looked over my lesson. Suddenly, I heard a loud whistle that echoed through the store. It was Uncle D standing in Thia's doorway signaling for me.

I made my way across the balcony and into the office. Don was sitting in Thia's chair with a large book and calculator. I also noticed a big pile of envelopes in two sections. Some were regular white envelopes while others were big manila ones.

Thia was leaning on the desk in front of me with her arms folded. Focus was sitting on the couch and Uncle D was standing at the door behind me. Everyone was focused on me, besides Don, who was engulfed in his activity. My mother initiated the discussion.

"Tell me about this white car that seems to be so interested in you?"

"Before I left this morning, it drove passed the house very slowly. I didn't see it again until I was standing at the bus stop in front of the library. It was parked across the street at the store."

"Alright, what happened when you got on the bus; did you see it again at all?"

At that moment, I knew Uncle D didn't mention Ms. L to Thia. I answered, "No Thia, I haven't seen it since."

"Did it make you feel threatened, August?"

"No, I just thought it was strange."

For the first time, I saw that Thia was uneasy and extremely pissed off. She snapped and told Focus to drive me to and from school until they found out what the fuck was going on! She ordered me to gather my things and hurry back. I did as she told me and spotted Mr. Phil closing up the store, so I decided to give him a hand. As I set my things on the bench by Thia's office door, I overheard her speaking.

"We have to use all of our powers to suppress this activity. Don, what's the count?" Thia snapped.

"I'll have it in a minute."

"Well speed it up. I'm ready to get out of here!"

Focus spoke up. "Our schedule is packed for the month and now we have a personal matter that may prove to be a threat to us?"

Uncle D cut in saying, "Thia, this was bound to happen sooner or later, we all knew that. We've been doing this dance since the early 80s and no matter how noble we think our cause is, this is still a town of extreme ignorance and envy. This always will be a place where it takes everything to get ahead. This is Baltimore City! This shit could've came from anywhere and they are trying to attack us at our weakest point, which is the Prince."

Thia shot back, "I don't give a fuck who it is." We will stop at nothing to destroy the threat! I'm calling the Pig to meet us here around 2 am.

Everyone agreed. Thia then said, "I have mixed emotions about August being initiated and it was for this exact reason."

"He is the best of us all," Uncle D added. "We all feel the same way but August is more than capable and with the proper training he could take the fraternity to new heights Thia. Plus, Don isn't a part of the pack."

"We need a Gray, Thia."

Focus agreed. "He's right, we do need a Gray and he's of age, you know that."

The room went silent for a few seconds until Thia spoke in conclusion. "Fine, we all agreed that only our blood is sacred and worthy to bear the ring. We will all play our part with August, but he is the pack's responsibility."

Focus agreed and said, "As the Alpha of the pack his initiation process will begin in February."

"What are you doing Prince?" Mr. Phil was at the bottom of the steps watching me eavesdrop. "Come here, man!"

I shot down the stairs and he immediately checked me. "You know better than that August, don't ever let me catch you doing that shit again! If they wanted you in there, they would call for you!"

"Yes sir, I got it."

"Now whatever you heard stays in my store alright!"

"Yeah, Mr. Phil."

"Good, now grab that broom and hit the floor will ya!"

I grabbed the push broom and got to it. Mr. Phil went back into his office to straighten up.

Chapter 11

I couldn't help but think about what I heard up there. The detail that stood out the most to me was when "The Gray" was mentioned. There wasn't a clue in my mind about what that was, and this is what they wanted me to be. We were three weeks into the new year and February was rapidly approaching. I still had two days to decide on it anyway but at their pace, the verdict may already be in for me. The office door shut and when I turned around, everyone was coming down the steps. Thia was the last one out as she locked the door. The lights went dim in the place. Mr. Phil could control the lights from his office. He then rushed to the door to unlock it for us. We all headed out onto Luzerne Street. Focus and Uncle D formed a two-man perimeter around the three of us to the house. When we got in, everybody went into the basement. Don and I sat on the couch and turned on the big screen.

Don said, "August, the family needs your help man."

I looked over at Don and asked, "How so?"

"I'm leaving for college soon and we have to stick together, you know."

"What can I do to help?"

"Things will change for you very soon as they did for me. It's for the better no matter how crazy shit may seem. Only your family knows what's best for you and the future of the bloodline."

"Keep it real with me Don. What the fuck is going on around here my nigga?"

"The world August! The world is a place that requires balance and that's what we represent. We don't conform to the times, but we do understand them clearly."

He switched the channel to CNN and told me to get to know the way of the politicians and their foreign policies.

"Understand what makes the world spin from the highest level to the very neighborhood you live in. Brains are the key to the game, and if you can think on your feet, then you'll have longevity. Only the strong survive out here, so take advantage of every opportunity. From here on out, I want your little ass out back with us lifting those weights."

Suddenly, there was a knock at the door. Don popped up and answered it. Neka walked in and greeted me before she kissed him and went upstairs. Afterward, Don sat back on the couch. Shortly after, everybody came up from the basement. Uncle D and Focus were prepared to head out as usual. Thia said goodnight to everyone and went upstairs. Don followed soon after, leaving me alone with the fellas.

As I watched TV, I felt the guys watching me. I turned to them both staring at me from the other side of the room. Focus was aggressively chewing his gum while Uncle D was pulling on his beard. They didn't say a word at all. I focused my attention back to the TV thinking about this weird routine my family had upheld ever since I could remember.

Thia speaks with these people at the end of every month and collects their envelopes. Then these two venture off into the streets in the heat of the night and do whatever the fuck they do! Even though I had school in the morning, I was determined to wait up on them tonight.

Now that I knew I had no choice, the only thing I could do was prepare for whatever was coming my way.

Focus demanded I grab a chair from the dining room and sit in front of them. I complied and found myself sitting before them. They both leaned forward and spoke in sync.

"What are you prepared to do for the family?"

"Anything," I sharply replied. A strong sense of approval washed over their faces as they went on.

"Are you a product of your environment or are you productive?"

"I'm productive to it."

"Do you realize that good and evil don't exist but choices do?"

"I do now."

"Do you believe in God?"

"Yes, I do."

Their eyes went towards each other.

Uncle D then asked, "Do you understand that nothing is controlling your life, actions or deeds except for the will that you possess?"

"Yes I do Uncle."

"August, your deeds will be the only thing tangible to determine your position in this life or the next."

Focus cut in. "August, what he's saying is that the time has come for you to abandon anything that will hinder you from doing what's necessary to suppress everything that threatens the balance we oversee. You're at the age now where you must learn our ways. It is a privilege for you to join the balance and run with the pack."

"Is Don a part of this"?

"Yes, August, but he organizes the revenue," Focus answered.

Uncle D shot back saying, "The two of you together will carry our agenda further than we ever could."

As they spoke, it dawned on me that I was very much needed. The fact that I was weak bothered them and I understood why my role was as important as they said it was. For some reason, the age of twelve was significant in my family and I figured this was as good a time as any to ask why.

"What does twelve mean?"

Thia interrupted, "Let me fellas! It should be me who explains this to him."

She appeared from the darkness in the hallway. I'm not sure how long she was standing there but it was clear that she was listening. I noticed her eyes were red and swollen as if she had just finished crying. She had mixed feelings concerning me from what I had heard in the office. Nonetheless, she still gathered the strength to let me know what it is herself.

"Twelve is not a number in this case baby boy, it's a symbol that represents the three realms of foresight. Separate the single digits of your age and add them together."

"I don't understand Thia."

"Yes you do, just add the one and the two and what do you get?"

"Three!"

She rubbed her hand down the back of my head repeatedly. A tear fell on her face as she said, "That's it, my son. In this life, you must read between the lines. This is also the fourth month since your birthday. Did you know that?"

"No."

"On September 18th you turned twelve, right?"

"Yes."

"Now it's January 22nd, four days past the four-month mark. 1/3 of 12 is 4 do you follow? In eight months, you'll be thirteen. This means you've already started the process with the book report you just finished recently. Everything we say and do is for a purpose. You will receive your next book in February, which is a very special month to us also. Hopefully, you can and will take what I explained to you seriously. Also never discuss what we've shared with anyone outside of the family, do you understand!"

"Yes, I do Thia."

"Take the rest of the month to yourself, August, and clear your head. February is the deadline for all the bullshit, you feel me?!"

I just nodded in agreement. She dismissed me with a firm goodnight!

Chapter 12

The ride to school the next morning was relaxing. It was nice and quiet. I guess Focus wanted me to clear my head. When we got to the library, I showed him the exact spot the car was parked in. He nodded and kept going. I wanted to see Nell, so I decided to speak up and asked him to drop me off around the corner.

"Hell no, your school is down the street!"

"I need to see my piece."

"Ya, piece! What the fuck August...you got a girlfriend?"

"Yeah, her name is Nell, and I go to her house every morning so we can walk together."

"Can I trust you, because last time I caught you and Nicci at the park and I had to halfway fuck y'all up!"

"I know better now."

"Great answer, where does she live?"

I directed him to her house and jumped out. As soon as I got through her basement door, her father was standing in the middle of the room. I was so shocked I couldn't move.

"Who the fuck are you, lil boy?!"

I back-peddled through the door and ran to school. Nell was absent for the entire day. After school, I stopped passed Ms. L's class and discussed what I learned. She was so impressed that she offered to help me on demand.

I walked outside to find Focus sitting on the hood of his car. I gave him a pound and told him what happened at Nell's house. As we were getting in the car, I noticed Nell's father glaring at me from across the street. He walked around his car in full stride towards me and I thought in my mind, "WRONG DAY Jack."

Focus slid across the hood of his Chevelle and stopped him in his tracks. The man ran straight into Focus and backed off when he felt that he was solid.

"I hope you weren't trying to get to my folks!" Focus said as his hand gestured back at me. "Because if you were, then you have a problem, don't you?"

The man looked at Focus like he was crazy and so did I. He was a big, black Jamaican guy and Focus was slim, but all muscle. Nell's father pointed at me and told Focus that I walked into his house this morning looking for his daughter!

"Hold on sir, where is your daughter?"

The man replied, "FUCK YOU BITCH!"

Focus grabbed the man by his genitals with his left hand and threw his right arm around his shoulders like they were hugging. The man let out a loud shriek and then vomited on the hood of the car. My jaw dropped, as I looked around to see if anyone had witnessed it, but it happened so fast that no one caught it.

Jenell got out of the car and ran towards me.

"August, what the fuck is going on?! Tell him to let my father go!"

Focus whispered something in the man's ear before letting him go. Nell's father fell on one knee with one arm on the hood of the car. Focus stood over him as if he had conquered Rome.

Nell asked, "Who the fuck is that August?!"

"He's my uncle."

She ran to her father's aid and said that she would call me later. Nell slid passed Focus with caution and helped her father to his feet. They made their way back to the car and got in. As they rode off the man shouted for me to stay away from his daughter and called me a punk!

Focus looked at me and shook his head and told me to get in the car. In the middle of our commute, he stopped at a local carry out where we sat down for a while to talk about what happened.

"August, you know this kind of shit can't happen right?"

"Yeah, I know it was a lot but this never happened before."

"Well, there's a first time for everything, and you can't go back there ever, do you know that?" I just shook my head.

"She's nice looking though, didn't know you like dark meat." I laughed and nodded.

"How long has she been your girl?"

"A few months or so."

"Are y'all fuckin!"

"Not yet, but I'm right there Focus, I know it."

"How do you know?"

"We are very comfortable around each other and I love her."

"I'm assuming Thia don't know shit about her?"

"Hell no!"

"Well, I'm not gonna dime you out, but I will say this. Don't pressure her, let that shit happen and don't mention sex at all, you feel me?"

"I want it just as bad as she does Focus."

"That's ok Prince, don't let her know that; believe me when it comes to these broads take ya time. You already got her, now play your position to the fullest."

I agreed with him of course. "Tell you what August, if she's willing to come see you, I will pick her up, but you better square it with Thia first, ya dig?"

"I understand Focus."

"You need to focus on the family. I will let you know when the time is right, but if she proves to be a distraction, she's gone, ya dig?"

"I got you Focus."

"You're a handsome little dude and the women will come, but you must choose wisely. Don't fuck all of them because you can, only the ones you can trust. Make sure she has her own plans and goals, that way she's not looking to come up off you. Don't associate yourself with these gutter rats and don't shit where you lay! People should never know who your girl is. Your woman is a reflection of you, so make sure you keep yourself at a certain status."

"I understand Focus, and I will remember that."

"Your choices reflect your family, so always represent us, Prince."

Chapter 13

We were two weeks into February and my house became a "chamber of secrets." Everyone was pitching in to bring me along. I became my family's project, but throughout all the pressure, I was determined to be the diamond. Academics was a major thing in my house and aside from me reading the book (Uncommon Sense), Thia was teaching me about the history of the country as well as its infrastructure. At this moment, I was studying the Louisiana Purchase of 1803 and the Missouri Compromise of 1820. Now the L.P. of 1803 was under the Thomas Jefferson administration. The land was purchased from France for $15 million at a rate of four cents per acre. The vast area extended from the Gulf of Mexico bounded west to the Rocky Mountains and north to the Canadian border. The M.C. of 1820 was about the House of Representatives passing a bill calling for the admission of Maine to the U.S.

since there were 11 free states and 11 slave states. The admission of Maine as a free state would upset the balance that was jealously guarded by all parties in the union. Therefore, the Senate adopted a bill that combined the admission of Maine with the admission of Missouri as a slave state.

All of this shit was boring to me as it should be to a twelve-year-old, but Thia took it seriously. She said that I must understand the way the United States was established and how I must learn to cross reference the origins of any and every topic of some importance. She informed me that these so-called prominent experts on the television along with teachers and professors will claim to know things and want you to take their word for it because of their academic status, but you will seek out the origins of it all.

Little did Thia know, I was already taking those steps with Ms. Larue as my private tutor. The fact that I was becoming smarter excited me. It also separated me from the neighborhood kids. Don't get it twisted though, I'd been in a few fights around the way and in school, but I knew how to keep shit quiet for the sake of my folks who hated bullshit. Bottomline, it was clear that I wasn't in the same category as everybody else. My folks weren't having it! Nell and I were always on the phone and it didn't seem to bother Thia as long as "I stayed on my shit" as she would say.

The phone was wedged between my ear and shoulder as I spoke to Nell. My body was completely sore from the workout routines the fellas had me on. Calisthenics one week and weight training every other week. My diet was closely monitored by Thia. Focus and Uncle D took fitness to the heart and they were very much inhuman as far as strength goes. Everybody was across the street at Phil's, and I had the house to myself. I had been trying to convince Nell to come over to my house for about an hour now. She was still hung up on the situation with Focus and how he *molested her father* as she liked to put it. Even though I haven't been back to her house since, we were still very much keeping our daily school visits between classes. I wrapped it up with Nell and hung up. Then I threw on my sweatsuit, boots, gloves, and hat and went out into the backyard to start my routine. I had a 30-minute burnout of pull-ups and dips. On weekends, we would run and I hated it! Focus would take us to Montebello Lake to sprint on a clock. I was fast as hell but to them, I had to be faster. I'm not ashamed to say I passed out on the track quite a few times, but failure was not an option! Saturdays were known as "The Pack Run." We ran individually as well as in a group and it was imperative that you kept up. Unfortunately, that was in two days, and I wasn't looking forward to it.

My routine ended and I sat on some crates to catch my breath. The conversation in the living room a few weeks ago was always in my thoughts. After I learned the significance of my age, February marked the beginning of the 2nd quarter of my age. I had no idea what was in store for me in the future, but I did know that I was being initiated this month at some point.

Gunshots broke the silence and my attention was captured as I counted them out. I tallied about 13 shots a few blocks over. About 10 minutes later, I could hear the sirens in the area. I remembered how Nicci boy and I would be fascinated with the sound of guns going off, but now I wasn't impressed at all. The older I got, the more I viewed life as a blessing every single day. Teddy bears, liquor bottles, and balloons were on almost every corner. People wore T-shirts bearing the faces of fallen soldiers with the same slogan on them. "The good die young" or "Gone but not forgotten." As fucked up as it was, a lot of them deserved it truthfully. Some of the shit these niggas were into called for their death. Uncle D came through the back door and joined me on the crates.

"Did you hear all the commotion just now?"

"Yeah, I was out here the whole time. It was about 13 shots from either a 40 or 45." Uncle shook his head and said, "That's a damn shame how you can identify the gun without seeing it August. Would you like me to tell you what I heard, Prince?"

"The same thing, right?"

"In a way yes, but the fact that it took 13 shots says what?" I just stared at Uncle D silently puzzled.

"It means that he was sloppy and his target saw him coming. If he wasted 13 shots then that means he chased him, which is too much work. When you're engaged with someone and it's life or death, they shouldn't see it coming, which leaves them no time to react."

"I was uncertain whether or not he was telling me how to kill somebody or if this was the way he would've done it. Either way I took it all in as a fun fact.

He summed it up with a jewel. "August life becomes easier with focus because our actions become habit. We also retain a purpose that will conform to our station in society. The higher we elevate, the more we can do. We are not conformist, meaning we do not live our lives by the rules of others. It also means that we will do what is necessary for us to do until we can throw off the chains of conformity."

I took a hot shower, ate and went to bed. The next morning, Focus dropped me off at school. I instructed him to pick me up at 3:30 because I had a session with Ms. Larue after school. Throughout the day, Nell and I did our thing between classes without incident. After the day was done, I reported to Ms. L's classroom like clockwork. I looked forward to Fridays for this moment only. I had honestly grown to respect Ms. Larue for helping me out. Most of all, it was nice that she even gave a fuck to keep her word. Plus, I still wanted to fornicate with her at any given moment. I took a seat at the round table in the back and waited for her to get off her cell phone.

While I was waiting, I took out my notes and went over our last week's lesson, which was the history of

Maryland itself. After a short while, she ended her call and joined me.

"Good Afternoon August; my apologies for holding us up. Give me a few minutes to get my coffee and I will be back so that we may begin."

She came back in and took a seat next to me. She started off: "Let's go over what we've learned on this topic."

I responded, "Well, Maryland's flag bears the arms of the Calvert and Crossland families. Calvert was the family name of the Lords of Baltimore who founded Maryland and their colors of gold and black appear in the 1st and 4th quarters of the flag. I also learned that the cross lands were the family of the mother of George Calvert, 1st Lord of Baltimore. The red and white Crossland colors, with a cross … appear in the 2nd and 3rd quarters."

"Ok August, I hear you; now tell me what year the flag was flown and why?"

"It was first flown on October 11, 1880 at a parade marking the 150th anniversary of the founding of Baltimore. It was also flown on October 25, 1888 at Gettysburg for ceremonies dedicating monuments to Maryland regiments of the Potomac Army. It wasn't adopted as the state flag officially until 1904."

"Outstanding August! You are definitely one of the brightest and most promising, let me tell you."

"Thanks Ms. L, I do appreciate it."

"August, can I ask you something if it's not too personal?"

"Yes mam?" I instantly pictured her throwing me across the desk and deflowering me. She went on. "There was a murder a few blocks from you last night. Were you anywhere in the area or did you hear anything?"

"No, but people get wacked all the time in my hood Ms. L so it's really nothing new at all."

She gazed at me for a second and said, "I see. How does your family react to the violence?"

"Truthfully, we all just mind our business and keep it moving, ya know?"

"I can understand that, but if you ever want to talk, I'm here, ok?"

"Yeah, Ms. L, thanks. If you don't mind me asking Ms. Larue, where are you from?"

"Potomac, Maryland, and yes, it is very upper class might I say!"

She turned her nose up as she made the statement, and we both just laughed. We went over my new lesson for a while and then I made my way home. That night I was in my room, l rolling up my weed. I climbed out onto the roof of the back porch. As I sparked up and allowed myself to zone out, the first thing that came to my mind was Ms. Larue. I could see that she was scared for me because of where I lived. It crossed my mind that she was probably helping me out on some charity shit, but if I was learning and becoming a better person, it really didn't make a difference. Then my family invaded my thoughts. The responsibility that was approaching rapidly had made me feel as though I wouldn't live up to what my folks needed me to be. At twelve years old, life shouldn't be so complex, but they believed in me so much that I had to be down for the cause.

While my thoughts raced, I took a look at my surroundings. Rats were running underneath the streetlights in the alley. There was an occasional dope fiend pacing, stalking the back streets on their nightly chase. The abandoned houses along Rose Street gave a grim testimony to the hostile environment. The biggest view of all was the landmark cemetery which stretched across the east side. I would always lose count when I tried to keep up with the tombstones. It always reminded me of how people are the only thing that matters in life and the true concept of family was to prolong the lives of one another by any means. At that moment it dawned on me that I would lie in this very cemetery for any of my loved ones or if need be, cast someone else's there without remorse.

Chapter 14

A loud bang on my bedroom door woke me from my sleep. I heard Uncle D shouting.

"PACK RUN!!"

He did the same to Don before he went back downstairs. I got up and threw on my sweatsuit dreading this day and all that came with it. It was the most intense training exercise known to man. Focus, Uncle D, and Don could run for hours, but I was determined to go the distance today. I grabbed my stopwatch and joined everyone in the kitchen. We couldn't eat until we got back, but we did drink raw eggs and water to stay hydrated. We took the Chevelle to the track and stretched as a unit on the field beforehand. We lined up on the track side by side with our watch set. Focus reminded us that we were starting with the two-mile jog at a graceful pace. We had to stay in a pack during the 1st mile, but the 2nd was a free run. We began on Focus' command and paced as a team. The 2nd mile came quickly and I slowed my pace up to practice the breathing technique that Uncle D taught me. Once I got to the finish line, I stood with the fellas to catch my breath before the lone sprint. After a short while, Focus instructed that the lone sprint was a test of individual endurance and stamina. He also said that whoever made the worst time would be chased by the pack. I already knew he meant me because my time was always the worst. It was freezing outside, and the sun was nowhere to be found. Don was up first. Uncle D was his shadow, which meant he had to catch Don in the middle of the mile to document any kind of fatigue Don displayed. Focus yelled, "MOVE!" and Don took off at full stride.

I watched as Don ate the track alive while Uncle D folded his arms as if he wasn't impressed at all. He reached the middle of the track and Focus told Uncle D to catch him! Uncle took off with strong strides and ended up at Don's side in no time. Uncle D studied Don all the way back to the finish line. As they passed the threshold, Uncle D slowed up in front of me and said, "Find yourself today. Let's get it, baby boy!"

Focus co-signed. I got back to the line and took my mark. Don still managed to taunt me as he was catching his breath: "3 minutes and 12 seconds rookie!" I just focused on the track ahead. The pact I made to myself last night suddenly came back into play. Focus yelled "Move Prince!"

I shot off as quick as I could. I reached the checkpoint and glanced at the finish line but saw nobody! I knew that very moment that I had become the "prey" in the infamous pack run! I looked over my shoulder and saw them all pursuing me. I instantly accelerated towards the finish line at my highest pace. Focus shouted, "Move Prince!"

I felt someone grab at the back of my neck which scared the shit out of me. I kept pushing full stride and approached the threshold. Within yards of it, focus shouted, "Keep moving August!"

We all shot passed the line and Focus took the lead about 5 paces in front of me. Uncle D appeared on my right while Don played the rear. My lungs began to burn, and the cold air formed a slight wheeze in my chest, but I knew that I couldn't stop. After about a quarter mile, Focus commanded "Prince, 3 lanes to my right now!"

I crossed Uncle D as he went left and Don shot into the middle. We all were at full speed. We kept that formation until Focus said, "Pair up!."

Uncle D shouted, "Get over here Prince!"

I switched lanes left and Uncle D pulled me in front of him while Don did the same with Focus. Don and I were clearly racing. Meanwhile, Focus and Uncle made sure we maintained our stride. At the last quarter mile and a half, Don and I were neck and neck.

Uncle D yelled: "August, take the middle lane now!"

As I accelerated passed Don, I took the middle lane and gave it all I could as I felt my body starting to give more and more.

Focus yelled, "Show me something Prince!" Uncle D followed up, "Find yourself August!"

I refused to be the weakest link. I pushed until my wheezing echoed through the entire park. All of them yelled, "Move!"

Uncle D laughed and said, "There he is!" The finish line was yards away and I heard Focus softly say, "Behold the Grey"

I cleared the threshold and kept going just to prove myself worthy of any respect the pack had for me. We ended up back home to finish our workout in the backyard. After my pull-ups came the dips. I came down and turned to watch the fellas doing what they did best. Focus was spotting Uncle D on the incline bench while he pressed the 100-pound dumbbells. Don was curling the 50-pound dumbbells. We had been out there for about 45 minutes and I was on my tenth set. After Uncle D got off the bench, he looked at me and snarled, "Fuck you waiting for?!"

I got back on my face and struggled with my 50 pushups. The routine destroyed me, but I made it through.

I paced around the porch relieved that this day had ended. The weight still applied pressure as it swung from the harness Don got me. I was getting stronger, and I could feel it. The steaming shower was a treat, and it became a habit to stretch underneath the water.

We all met up at the kitchen table for dinner and crashed after.

Ten days had passed since the pack run.

As we were eating, Thia snapped at me. "Wassup with this girl calling my house, August?!"

Everybody turned to me at once anticipating my answer. I looked at Thia and said, "She's good people."

She just studied me for a minute. "So, I'm guessing she's from school, huh?"

"Yeah, and I try to walk her home every day."

"Do you try or is that what you do?"

"Yeah, I walk her home."

"Ok, I just wanted you to know the difference between trying and doing, you feel me?" I nodded and kept eating.

"You know if you're having sex, I gotta fuck you up right?!" Everybody at the table laughed except for me and of course her.

"Did you hear me?"

"Yeah, Thia I heard you."

"So, answer the question boy!"

"No, we didn't have sex yet."

"Good, now I'm not stupid. I know it will happen eventually and it may not be with this girl, but I need you to understand that pussy clouds your reasoning; believe me, I know. Women…we lie about everything, and we don't care who we hurt as long as we get our way. We will smile at you, tell you we love you and let you think whatever game you're running is working without showing our hand. So, make sure trust is the first line of establishing anything. If you have a girl you can trust, that's good. Even if she has some shit with her, there's always time to mold her properly.

"But if the bitch has no spine, she's always complaining with her hand out and reminding you of what she's done for you, then you already know that she will do anything to get ahead in life. Stand clear of the ones who crave attention. Also, the best ones are not the best looking, remember that."

Focus stepped in with, "A woman will only be as good as her man is. So carry yourself with respect and keep it real with yourself first. You can't be real with anyone else if you're not real with you."

They all meant well and I knew that. One thing was certain though: whenever they spoke and no matter what we discussed, I was always receptive.

It was the last morning of February and Don and I were getting ready for Bella to pick us up in the van within the next hour. After I had gotten dressed, I took a seat at my desk to memorize my vocab words in order as Uncle D demanded. He gave them to me Friday night and told me it was imperative to memorize them ASAP. We sat at the table as a family and Thia couldn't keep her hands off of me. She was brushing my hair and fixing my clothes as if she were nervous about something. While I ate, she stared at me as if I were a newborn again. When we finished, Don and I went to sit on the front stoop.

"How do you feel today, August?" I gave him a weird look as he put his arm around me and pulled me into him. He said, "Just listen to me. I've watched you grow from a kid into a young man and you're smarter than I was when I was your age."

"But Don, you are going to college soon."

"Yeah, but I don't mean it that way. A, your destiny is far greater than mine. The kind of wits you have are foreign to me. Everything will make more sense very soon. August, just promise me something."

"What's that?"

"Regardless of what people believe or say to you. No matter what position you find yourself in by an adversary who seems invincible from all angles. Never let this world or anything in it sway your heart away from the resilient agenda of your blood."

The van pulled up and we were off. Once we got to church, service began immediately. Don's words resonated with me, and I tuned everything else out until Bella got up for testimony to speak on Don's transition to Penn State. I watched as she poured herself out to the church about the works and wonders of God.

After the day had ended, we waited for the van to come back and get us after its first trip. There were a few of us left in the church. Bella and I were sitting in the lobby catching up on my week.

"How's school my love?"

"I enrolled in an afterschool program."

"Good boy August, always do something constructive with your spare time. What's the program about?"

"World history and the origins of U.S. customs and traditions."

"Wow you are smart A, but don't neglect your bible, ya hear?"

"Yes ma'am. Can I ask you a question Bella?"

"Always love."

"What's your definition of family and how do you maintain the bond between us?"

She took a minute and scanned me before she started in.

"Family is the foundation that your morals, principles and values originate from. The decisions you make as an adult are molded by the lessons you learn in your home. When one of us chastises you for a bad choice you've made, it's to develop your common sense. What keeps your family together is compromise; you need to be able to meet each other halfway in times of strife. Take your brother as a fine example of raising the status of us all. I had to scrub white folks' floors with a bucket and a sponge while Althia watched. Bottom line, I did whatever I had to do to support my family with no regrets and that is reassured thanks to Don making something of himself."

She was overjoyed about Don. It was almost like she was going to Penn State, and in a way, she was. We arrived at the house at 10 and Uncle D was standing in the doorway. Don kissed Bella and got out of the van. When I hugged Bella, she whispered to me, "Whatever your family needs you to do, August, make it well within your means to show your devotion and support to get it done baby."

We said goodnight to everyone and headed inside. The house was spotless as usual and cinnamon was boiling on the stove in Thia's old pot. The smell was intoxicating beyond belief. I was spent, so I headed upstairs and took a shower. When I got out, I went straight into my room and laid my school clothes out before I crashed. I assumed that everybody was in the basement, so I went over my words for about five minutes and went to sleep.

The alarm clock went off suddenly. It felt like I had just fallen asleep. When I rolled over to shut the clock off there was a shadowy figure standing at my window which scared me stiff.

"Turn off the clock Prince."

It was Uncle D. I got up and hit the button and saw that it was 11:30 pm. I sat down on the bed as my eyes adjusted to the darkness. Uncle D had taken down my blinds and curtains while I was asleep. His hands were around his back as he focused on the full moon above the graveyard. The light from the moon shined on him and gave him a majestic vibe.

"It's time nephew," he softly said.

I already knew what he meant.

"After tonight August, your journey of understanding about what the family is truly about will be well underway." He paused for a few seconds. "I need to know that you are ready for what comes next and if you in any way feel pressured into this."

"No Uncle, I'm willing and able to join the family and whatever comes next, we will deal with as a family".

He turned to me and said, "That is an outstanding answer August and the honor is all mine to inform you that everyone is waiting for you downstairs. Take some time and go over your words. When I call for you, come on down, nephew."

He left out and shut the door behind him. The moonlight provided enough light for me to go over my assignment. I was surprisingly calmer than I thought I would be. I stood at the window and saw the biggest and brightest moon I had ever seen. Didn't have a clue of how symbolic it was. However, finding out would be the answer to many of my questions. My thoughts were racing and everything came to me at once from Bella to Nell, Ms. Larue, Nicci boy down to when I saw Tank and Gamo get killed five years ago. I knew that everything had led up to this very moment. Every conversation, every experience, and everything I had learned along the way was preordained for this.

Uncle D opened the door and said, "Let's get you straightened out." He instructed me to take off my shorts and tank top. "Only your briefs, Nephew."

This was some weird shit, I thought to myself. I took everything off except for my briefs. He asked if I had to use the bathroom because the initiation couldn't be interrupted whatsoever. I went and tried for the sake of that alone. When I was done, he met me in the hall with an American flag bandana. He then blindfolded me with it and said, "Follow me Prince."

He put his hand on my shoulder and guided me down the stairs. My heart pounded because this felt more and more like some cult shit. The fact that Don went through this blew my mind or maybe this was reserved for me only, who fucking knows. We made it to the bottom and turned right towards the kitchen. Even with the blindfold on, I could tell the house was extremely dark as the smell of cinnamon lingered in the air. Uncle D opened the basement door and guided me down the steps after he shut it behind him. My pulse bolted like thunder throughout my entire body as we descended into the only area I had never explored in my own home. He squeezed my shoulder a bit and told me to relax.

His voice calmed my anxiety along with the thought of my family seeing me through it all. When we reached the bottom, I could feel carpet under my bare feet until I felt a dirt like substance all of a sudden. Once I was in position, I felt his hand leave me as he whispered, "Remember your words in correct order."

I stood in silence for a while before I heard Thia's voice. "August McMann Joyner, born September 18th 1987, son of Ronda Althia Fleetwood and Cain McMann. Tonight will be a test of intellect, vigilance, and devotion to a cause that you will be sworn to adopt and uphold from this night forward. The pit that you are standing in is known as the silver circle. It symbolizes the exile of ignorance which is a commitment to the 1st realm of foresight from slavery into liberation. Learning to exhaust, eliminate, and bring decay to all knowledge and beliefs which are not beneficial. Allowing your voice of reason to bring all things into question and challenge, one must produce stats of intellect through studies and assigned reports with good results in order to advance. All distractions and outside influences are extinguished once selected by the fraternity. Knowledge should be applied to your everyday life. Our way is all that exists and is the sole purpose why we seek refuge in our own. Those who are not initiated into the group will be viewed as part of the problem from which our will is the solution. By conforming to the group's cause you will denounce all forms of ignorance and all ideologies of control. Nothing diverts your thoughts, choices, or deeds but you. The actual existence of choice and free will is highlighted in the group. The concept of right and wrong is merely a state of mind, but intention is what distinguishes higher self from lower self. Once understanding of oneself is obtained, one will become liberated with the light and refer to your old ways as the dark ages. Do you understand?"

"Yes, I do."

"The blindfold represents the lies, deceit, and false concepts of control this country has casted upon you to hinder you from doing what's necessary to raise the status of your community as well as your people. Do you believe in God?"

"Yes."

"Good, because God is very real. However, organized religion has divided the people by debate of which source is the purest. We believe and recognize a higher power and creator of all things, but we will not participate in manmade religions. Let our deeds show that the compassion we have for the people justifies our means of making a difference to all who are oppressed. And do you accept this responsibility?"

"Yes, I do."

Before she went on, I was besieged by heat. It intensified as I stood quietly. Thia's voice broke the silence. The last minute of this day before the midnight hour symbolizes your initiation into the first realm. This is the test of intellect: on the 28th day of the 2nd month you are faced with 12 questions of which you already have the answers.

"In order to hear them you must create twelve only with the numbers I mentioned beforehand. You have 60 seconds to make twelve from 28 and 2."

She left me in silence once again. I was confused beyond belief because 28 and 2 was 30 when added together and if you subtract it was 26. This made no sense at all to me.

She shouted, "30 seconds!" Due to the heat, I was sweating profusely.

"25 seconds," she shouted!

I took time to do the math in my head before I spoke up: "I have it."

"Let's hear it then!"

I said: "2 +8 equals 10, plus 2 is 12."

"Very good August, things are not always what they seem, would you agree?"

"Yes, I would."

"Now you must choose your words wisely and answer the twelve questions of your initiation into the silver circle."

I thought to myself that she had to be referring to the vocabulary words that I was instructed to memorize. Other than that, I was clueless. She began by saying: "August, at this midnight hour you must answer the following questions in order. Again, I advise you to use your vocabulary wisely."

The questions began:

Thia: Immortality is obtained by?	Me: Intellect
Thia: Love dwells ithin?	Me: Loyalty
Thia: Reality is ruled by?	Me: Reason
Thia: Promise is kept for	Me: Purpose
Thia: Honesty is upheld	Me: Honor
Thia: Lies are only true if you?	Me: Listen
Thia: Vision is preserved for the?	Me: Vigilant
Thia: Fidelity is reserved for your?	Me: Family
Thia: Tyrants are tamed through?	Me: Treachery
Thia: Protection is provided for the?	Me: People
Thia: Morals motivate?	Me: Morality
Thia: Justice is always?	Me: Justified

"The questions are a pledge to the fraternity and the answers are a testimony of what it will take to uphold our way. This will be known to you only as the "Pillars of

Promise." If you should ever find yourself in a moral dilemma behind any deed which was placed upon you by the fraternity, always refer back to the pillars that we stand on and the promise we've made to keep our foundation indestructible no matter what. Understand?"

"Yes, I do."

"Now remove your blindfold, August!"

I pulled it off to find myself standing in a homemade pit of dirt with rocks surrounding it in a perfect circle holding the dirt in place. There was fire in a shallow trench along the outside of the rocks as well. When I tried to scan the room, it was pitch black. I couldn't even see who was speaking to me or where they were. I looked above me to find a bucket hanging upright over my head by a nail in the ceiling. I was drenched in sweat. The fire wasn't close enough to burn me, but it almost felt like it.

Focus spoke from the darkness. "The pit you're standing in symbolizes the dirt that we do to further our agenda, the dirt we came from which represents our environment, and the dirt we will return to once the dust leaves our bones."

Uncle D then spoke. "The fire represents the turmoil and ambition of our adversaries that surround us each and every day."

Thia added, "This is a test of your vigilance. Put out the fire my son!"

I immediately grabbed the bucket and walked towards the edge of the circle. I started to pour the water onto the fire to find that the flames had grown higher and more violent. I jumped back more frightened than I had ever been. The bucket was filled with gasoline.

Thia said, "I thought we agreed that things aren't what they seem August."

My eyes gazed into the darkness for a while before I placed the bucket back onto the nail above me. The temperature was rising, and my confusion clouded my judgment.

Focus softly said, "The dirt we do Prince."

I looked to my feet and understood the concept of how the dirt we do furthers our agenda to put out the fire in our enemies. I started to take handfuls of dirt and cast it onto the fire. It worked as the flames died with the more dirt I added. Finally, it was fully extinguished as I stood exhausted in darkness. I heard Focus say, "There's a diamond."

Thia appeared in front of me and lit a small candle. She said, "Look on the ground son."

She laid the candle in the circle so I could see clearly. There was a scroll that was buried beneath the dirt and I picked it up. Once I stood, she grabbed her candle from the circle. Then I saw Uncle D, Focus, and Don, join her surrounding me with lit candles.

She said, "At this time, my son, allow the light provided by your family to be enough for you to take your vow of silence. This is the final test of devotion."

I opened the scroll and held it at both ends and she said, "Please begin."

I started the oath: "Our society is completely engulfed in silence, secrecy, and solitude. The anatomy of the fraternity should never be revealed to any "parts of the problem." The initiates are imprisoned under the "Missing Tongue." We should never appear in any place in our own name. Our agenda should always be hidden within another agenda, aimed in the opposite direction. Our way is a powerful agent to the uninitiated and may precipitate a media avalanche. Members of the society are of the most disciplined stature and wealthy with confidence within the society. The Missing Tongue is a concept of oral chastity valued by those who vow never to give testimony concerning the revelations of our way. Dare we never disclose, for the point of the tongue will bring Qarma against those…"

There were two questions at the bottom along with the answers. Focus asked the first one. "Cause will determine?"

I answered, "The Qarma."

Uncle D asked the second. "While greatness comes graceful to…?"

I answered, "The group."

They all blew out their candles at once leaving me in darkness once again. I heard my mother sniffling as she let out a soft whimper. **"Welcome home August!"**

Chapter 15

I poured Thia another shot of Remi Martin in her glass on the wooden desk, while Mrs. Riley explained her vendetta to Thia.

"He's been dangerous since he was little. Always into things around the neighborhood and causing ruckus. He's become undesirable to us all with no signs of slowing down."

Thia interrupted. "Tell me about the situation Mrs. Riley and I will see what I can do for you and your family."

"Oh ok, well he shot my grandson for no apparent reason. Jake asked him not to sell drugs in front of my house out of respect and he shot him in his mouth. Mind you, he watched Jake grow up in that house on that very block."

"Yeah, we heard, sorry about that. How's Jake?"

"He's just fine; the hospital will release him some time this month. They had to get the bullet out of his throat, so it took longer than expected."

"What did the police say?"

"Nobody came forward and of course, Jake didn't speak up either, but it's better this way. I will put my faith in you, besides we worked together before with good results."

Thia leaned back in her chair and nodded in agreement with her. Focus sat on the couch on the other side of the room while Uncle D sat outside the door to ensure that there would be no interruptions. Don was behind the desk to her right with his head in the books as usual. I just leaned up against the wall in the corner behind Don and listened. Mrs. Riley gave Thia the envelope and she passed it to Don.

"How much is it?" Thia asked.

"It's about 4500; this weekend I'm going to bingo night. I could have another five hundred then."

"That won't be necessary at all; this is fine Mrs. Riley. What are you requesting of me exactly?"

"Well…" Then she paused for a minute. Focus lifted his head from the newspaper in anticipation. Mrs. Riley asked my mother if she could tell her in her ear. Thia came from around the desk and leaned over. We all tried to tune in but still nothing. Thia leaned up and said "Well, Ms. Thang, I will see to it, you here."

"Thank you, Althia, really."

"Alright, have a good day, Mrs. Riley."

After she left, Uncle D came in and said, "That's the last of them."

Thia stood still with her hands on her hips in relief, while Uncle D shut the door and took a seat. Focus asked, "What is it that she wanted?"

She shook her head and said, "She wants us to cut his nuts off!"

My jaw dropped as my arms unfolded. Everybody else just shook their heads in disgust.

Don replied, "She's worse than these niggas are."

There were 14 envelopes in the basket in front of Don on the desk. Some white, others brown. Don separated fifties and hundreds and started the money machine. The rest of the bunch were in deep conversation. I wasn't really hands-on yet, so I was instructed to observe for the last month just to learn the ways of the group first. Since my initiation, Uncle D was teaching me how to fight, while Focus had been taking me under highway bridges to show me how to shoot. I had grown stronger from the workouts over time, and it showed in certain areas, especially cardio. We were set to have a "Think Tank" that evening when we got home. That's where we dialogued about past lessons or present. We also came up with solutions to small quarrels in the area. We always presented our own perspectives. While they convened the meetings at Phil's, I would get the guests drinks or made sure everyone was comfortable in the room. One thing is for certain though-- I could not voice my opinion or speak at all in this room. I was definitely a part of the fraternity, but I wasn't initiated into the pack as of yet. Thia was the matriarch of the group and the "moon" to the pack. A few days after my initiation, Thia explained what the group was all about. We had a one-on-one at the round table in the basement.

"August, allow me to explain what everyone's role is in the fraternity. I'm the matriarch, and that's a woman who dominates or rules a family or group. The group was founded in February of '79. I was 11 years old. We were still living in the projects then and times were different. Your uncle was a street fighter or a regulator as we called him. I was off the chain as well. We were younger and didn't have a clue of how to control our emotions. Focus was from Jefferson Street. He's our first cousin on Patti's side of the family. He was known as a killer even back then. Fredrick earned the name Focus because he had narrow vision on all of his victims. He could also spot any situation that might escalate or had the potential to.

All three of us were influential in the hood and people feared us a great deal. Education from the ex-Black Panthers showed us that our power should be used to help others find comfort in our fucked-up surroundings. So, we put our heads together in the courtyard one day and vowed that we would keep the pigs out of our community by policing it ourselves. Even though I had a nasty attitude, the fellas thought that it would help to develop my people skills if I became the one to hear out the community's problems.

Now at that time, I didn't believe in standing for people who didn't stand up for themselves, but in time, it made me a better person. It gave me a purpose to strive and educate myself. Now the fellas have a special talent for keeping people in order and they always make good on my promises to the community. We made quite a bit of money too and invested it back into the projects with a series of home improvement projects. We even helped send a few to college.

You see, August, no one will help us but us, baby boy. We have to play our part with each other and get rid of whoever tries to dull the faith of the people with their bullshit mentality. Remember if you shit on folks on your way up, you'll surely eat it all on your way back down. Everything has a counterpart. What goes up must come down and that's what we are. Night and day. That's what we represent because we dig for gold within people, but we are prepared to deal with the dirt they might have on them. Understand? However, the real enemies are the motherfuckers who make the laws that trap us all in the long run. These people's idea of a solution is to stuff us in concentration camps or prisons and keep the drug trade alive. A clear case of cause and effect. The drugs don't get in this country by itself and prisons are a multi-billion-dollar business. As you get older, you'll understand. The more you study your enemy, the better your chances of survival are. You and Don will be the ones to raise the family to a status that we could only dream of."

I asked, "Why do they call you the moon?"

"Well, it's few reasons, but I've learned that I shine even in the darkest of places. I'm always in control of the tide within my community. Through intellect, perseverance, wisdom, and sentiment, my soul is illuminated. What you must also understand about the moon is that it takes in between 28-29 days to become full circle and it is at its most radiant state. It has a symbolic relation to women as well. This is why I wear white when dire circumstances are brought to me because no matter how bad the situation may seem, I will always pull everything towards the light and expose it."

After we finished up at Phil's, we packed up and went home for the evening. As soon as we were done with dinner it was time for our "Think Tank" in the basement. I enjoyed the discussions we had down there. It opened my understanding of life to a whole new perspective and it gave me a chance to level with my loved ones.

The basement was like a lounge / sanctuary or hall that was devoted to the group. There was an expensive black velour rug that covered the majority of the floor. There was a black, leather loveseat sofa in the middle of the basement along the wall. There was a wooden coffee table in the center of the loveseat that had Q.G. engraved in the middle. On the opposite side of the room was a built-in bar with wooden stools around it. Our photos were framed and placed above the bar. Me and Don's photos were beneath everyone else's to separate the generations. The room behind the bar was the laundry room and it also had another bathroom with a shower included. Finally, there were pictures of Black leaders along the walls of the basement: Malcolm X, Dr. King, Stanley Williams, George Jackson, Huey Newton, James Carr, Winnie Mandela, Larry Hoover, and Ellsworth "Bumpy" Johnson, among others. The frames aligned throughout the basement leading toward the center above the couch. In between them hung a black velour banner with golden letters that read: The Fraternity of Family.

There was money spread across the coffee table while Don did the books. Thia made herself comfortable in the center of the couch below the banner while Focus and Uncle D sat on stools at the bar. I was behind the bar preparing everyone's drinks. After I slid the fellas their glasses, I placed both the coaster and drink on the table in front of Thia and took a seat beside her. Focus sipped his drink and said, "Before we start, does anyone have any pics?" This was short for problems, issues, or concerns. When no one spoke up he went on.

"Alright, tonight wc will spcak on the strategy that our enemies use to break down the family establishment in this country. Let's start with the role of the father. As the man, it's his duty to provide for the entire family so he works for the better part of the day and makes it to the table in time for dinner every night. However, over the course of time, his body is torn from the labor until he's physically weak. Men of color often use their bodies to make a living instead of their minds. Bottom line, the local school system is designed to set us up to work jobs and not seek out a career. Now we can't blame the system for everything; we take part in our own downfall as well by choosing to be ignorant. The opportunity to better yourself is always there, but it starts with the household first. The sad truth to this story is that our people have been robbed of our culture and identity. So, we try to fit or adapt to this country's traditions without knowing the true origins from which they came. Our last names are that of our slave masters, and we cannot speak our native tongue whatsoever. So as a family, we must first break the ugly trend within our own house before we can help anyone else who may still be enslaved to it."

I listened as Focus spoke with so much charisma and obvious concern for the state of our people as a whole. But I couldn't help but hear him zero in on Blacks only so I asked, Are we a racist fraternity?" Everyone stopped talking to direct their attention towards me.

"No," Uncle D said. "We are not racist because we aren't the only ones who fall victim to this system. There are whites, Italians, Irish, Jamaicans, Latinos, and Mexicans who face the same social issues as well. But what distinguishes us from the rest of them is the fact that they have their own identity because they still practice their own culture and traditions. We all might be in the same ocean, but at least they know where their boats sailed from."

I nodded in agreement.

Thia took over stating, "This subject is very delicate on so many levels due to the cause that we stand for. We always hold family in high regard because life is meaningless without one another. Blood will indeed double-cross you just as fast as anyone else but that's due to a lack of discipline, outside influences, or addictive vices. This is what the system feeds off and how it exploits weak links within the chain. I would willingly die or spend my life in captivity to preserve any one of you. We all must stay on the same page in the book of our bloodline concerning the history that we make in the generations to come."

Don interrupted, "Twenty-five thousand in total."

Uncle D and Focus took the money into the laundry room and changed their clothes. Don sat back in his seat and unloosened his tie. Thia was writing on her pad in silence. I grabbed the empty glasses and made myself useful. Once I got behind the bar, the guys were coming out of the back. I poured them two small shots and they downed them before slamming the glasses back onto the bar. Focus walked towards Thia and retrieved the piece of paper from her then examined it thoroughly. Once he memorized it, he said in a firm voice, "You're with us tonight, Prince!"

Don lifted his head from the back of the couch in a shocked manner and blew the weed smoke out rapidly. My mother anxiously objected, "No! It's too early, he's not ready yet!"

Uncle D replied, "He is as ready as he will ever be and it is time for him to take his place in the pack."

Before Thia could get another word out, Focus grabbed both of her shoulders and said,

"At this rate he will never be ready; now, we understand how you feel but a person in your position must not display this level of emotion at a crucial moment. Wouldn't you agree?"

She pulled herself together. Focus commanded me to go and get dressed! Uncle D ordered me to follow him into the back. I shut the door behind me. He turned to me and then got on one knee as if he were proposing. He placed his left hand behind my neck pressed his right up against my chest and felt my heart racing.

"Listen to me, Prince. Your test tonight requires no emotion of any kind, just training and instinct. Let that anxiety and adrenaline heighten your senses and bring you the strength to see you through this."

"I'm scared Uncle D."

"You should be, but after tonight fear won't be useful." He got up and reached into the closet and pulled out a bag. He threw it to me and told me to put it on.

I reached inside and snatched out a smoke gray medium sweatsuit and pair of dark gray and black leather gloves. It also contained a smoked gray hat and facemask. I got undressed and put on the uniform. I noticed Uncle D and Focus had on black ones.

We came from the back and the basement was empty. The both of us made our way upstairs to find Focus standing in the backdoor threshold. I walked into the backyard as Uncle D opened the gate and disappeared into the alley. Focus and I stood quietly for a while.

Suddenly, I heard the sound of glass breaking. After a few times it stopped, and the alley went extra dark. He had busted the streetlights out completely. Focus led me out into the alley without a word. Uncle D came out of the shadows and said, "Focus and I are going into the field while you make the plot for us."

Focus picked me up and told me to grab the wall. I reached out to grab the ledge and climbed up on the cemetery wall. I jumped over and the two of them followed behind me. They led me as we walked along the wall for about 3 minutes until I spotted a shovel stuck in the dirt.

Focus instructed me to get the shovel and dig! They walked off and left me to it. Before they got too far, I asked, "How deep?"

Without turning around Uncle D responded, "Deep enough to hide a secret."

I began to dig once I saw them jump the wall. I already knew that someone was going into this hole. After 10 minutes of digging, my thoughts began to overwhelm me. I wondered if this was meant for me or was I just trying to please my family.

What are we really a part of? Is my family manipulating me into being a killer? Can I actually kill somebody when the time comes? How could this truly help us as a community or a people as a whole? My mind was all over the place but my frustration fueled my will to dig and I was now standing inside the plot casting dirt over my left shoulder. My back began to tighten up, my arms were burning, and I was out of breath all at the same time. I threw the shovel down and sat in the dirt. The reality of the situation didn't dawn on me until I gazed into the black sky from the grave. *This shit is crazy*, I thought. I have got to be the only twelve-year-old doing this shit right now! The hole was probably 3 ½ feet deep and about an arm's length wide. For some reason, I began to pray: *God, thank you for my health and strength, thank you for my life and all that is good in it. Forgive me for the sins that I've committed in the past and forgive me for the sins I will commit in the future. Please grant me the grace of your light at my darkest hour and bless the souls of those who have perished and lie here in this very place…. amen.*

"Are you quite done?!" I stood up and turned to find Focus standing over top of me.

"Yeah, I'm done."

"August what the fuck are you doing in there?"

"I was taking a break."

"So, you decided to sit there? Your little ass is fucking strange do you know that?"

"I guess so Focus." He reached his hand out and pulled me from the pit.

"Not bad," he said while he examined my work.

"Are you ready for this baby boy, because we're counting on you. I'm sure you've had a lot of time to think about it, am I right?"

I didn't respond.

He led me to a tomb made of stone that you could walk into. The rough texture had been smoothed and polished to give it that modern look. It stood about ten feet tall with a dome on top of it. There were two pillars at both corners of the entrance. The door was black with a gold handle on the right of it that stretched vertically. The tomb was custom made and in plain view from my bedroom window. I would always overlook it as I counted the tombstones from the roof.

Focus softly stated, "The majority of what you've been taught has led up to this night. The purpose of the pack is to maintain order. The people keep us in power by investing into our promises with results. No matter how bad things get, don't ever give up on the people, Prince."

"I got it Focus."

"Good, now when you walk into this tomb you will demonstrate how tyrants are tamed through treachery. This is one of those times where you might seem confused about the deed that is asked of you, but you must remember that reality is ruled by reason and justice is always justified. Don't get it fucked up for we are carnivores, and our purpose is to devour anything that threatens the balance!"

He walked to the door and placed his left hand around the handle. "Say the word, Prince."

I stalled for a full minute while he studied me with anticipation. I took a deep breath and told him to open it. He let go of the handle and walked up to me. He leveled his face with mine and said, "A man creates his conditions, so open it up yourself Prince."

He stepped aside as I made my way to the door and grabbed the handle to pull.

"Slide it to the left!" He said.

The door was heavy, so I had to use my right shoulder to help push the door to the left. It was pitch black inside. I felt Focus place both hands on each of my shoulders as he guided me in.

"Step down Prince!"

I walked down three steps before he turned to slide the door shut. I couldn't see my hands in front of me, it was so dark. I heard a match striking behind me. When I turned around, Focus was lighting a lamp and hung it on a hook to the left of the door. He lit another and hung it on the opposite side illuminating the tomb. He pointed behind me and I turned to find Uncle D leaning on the wall at the rear of the tomb with a naked man sitting on the floor. Both arms were fully extended as he laid strapped to the cement bench. His head was hunched over as if he were unconscious. His legs were spread apart as well. Uncle D and he had an unsettling look in his eyes.

"Don't worry, he'll be awake any minute; we chloroformed him. But when he wakes up, you will see to it that he meets his demise."

I turned to Focus as he went on. "His bones symbolize the wall of innocence that you need to tear down in order to become the gray wolf and complete the pack."

"Why Focus?"

Uncle D let out a loud sigh as if he were pissed off. He then snapped at me. "August, we do not question the balance, nephew! Everything is arranged by the moon and carried out by the wolves. We don't shed the blood of the innocent, but we do prey on the motherfuckers who victimize good people. They came to us because half the police in the city are working for the cartels or are too incompetent to solve cases. August, we are their only option down here and we intend to keep it that way!"

"So, we play God then?" I replied.

"Not at all! We are not in that business Prince, but these people pray until they're blue in the face waiting for something to happen every day. We choose to answer them and honor their faith with our works. It's easy to remain silent and not speak up about the bullshit. It's easy to mind your business and let these motherfuckers flex on the weak, but it's hard to stand up for what you believe in. It's hard to bring peace to a hostile situation. It's hard to tell the truth in a circle full of liars. Bottom line, if you can't deal with a problem as small as this, how the fuck will you combat a system that oppresses us by the millions?!"

Focus followed up, "This is not a fucking conundrum Prince! Do you know who that is?"

"Who?"

"Go ahead and pull the bag off of his head."

I snatched the bag off and stood in shock. It was Riley; he was a heavy hitter in the smack world. He controlled Zone 18 as far as heroin goes. He was a rich nigga and untouchable, so he thought. He started to come to slowly, but surely.

"There he is," Focus said sarcastically. We all gave him a moment to grasp the dire situation.

As he clung to life he said, "What the fuck is this, some satanic shit! Who the fuck is you niggas supposed to be? You freak motherfuckers got me naked and shit, I hope y'all ain't tryna fuck!"

He was hilarious, but we were dead serious. Focus spoke up, "Riley from Normal Street, how ya doin' brother?"

"Yeah, that's me G!"

"Tonight, you will pass away sir."

He hung his head and said, "Whatever they're paying you, I will triple it my nigga. I'm worth $750,000 right now and I got it on deck!"

"It's not about the money Riley, this is an initiation." He was puzzled beyond relief.

"If this ain't about the money then what?"

"Your deeds landed you here, and you've become a problem for your people. An eleven-year-old overdosed last month, right?"

"My nigga, I don't control who buy my shit. He was a dope fiend so fuck him!"

"That's why you're here."

"If you get ya rocks off killing drug dealers then y'all got your work cut out for you. This is "body more" and there will always be another me!"

"Then it's safe to say that you'll have plenty of company where you're going because we will always be here as well."

He was speechless and so was I. I wanted to get it over with quickly, but with my family, things were never that simple.

"August, my boy, it's time to tear that wall down!"

Riley looked at me. "A kid? You people are worse than me turning a kid out on murder! You motherfuckers are hypocrites!"

Uncle D said, "No…we are family."

Then he slammed a sledgehammer onto the cement bench behind his head causing him to jump on impact. He rested both hands on the rubber handle as he balanced it vertically on the bench.

"What the fuck is that?!" Riley shouted.

"The weapon of choice sir; karma can be very heinous."

"Just shoot me man."

"Don't make a big deal out of it, August, grab the hammer!"

Uncle D handed it to me and came from around the bench. We traded places, and now I was facing the back of Riley's head. They grabbed his ankles and held him in place. Riley started to pant loudly.

"Break every bone in his body, but leave his skull intact," Uncle D commanded.

"What?" I replied.

"Turn his bones into dust, Prince!"

"Oh, shit," Riley shouted! "Help me some fucking body!"

Focus talked over him. "Nobody can hear him at all, trust me!"

I twisted my palms back and forth to tighten my grip. I raised the hammer like an ax and paused. I watched as fear overcame Riley. He squirmed trying to free himself without a chance.

He turned toward me as much as he could and snapped, "Fuck you, pussy butt ass nigga! I have been getting money since you were pissing on ya nuts! I've been out here long enough to see you ain't got it in you lil August! You are not built for this shit!"

Uncle D lunged and slapped him on his forehead, sending his head bouncing off the cement bench. Uncle D gave me a sinister look and I knew that if it didn't mean anything else it meant that it was time for me to commit. I brought the hammer down as hard as I could and missed. The hammer cracked against the cement inches away from his elbow. Uncle D came around the bench and adjusted my grip, putting my right hand further up the handle to guide it correctly. When he backed away, I dropped the hammer again smashing his forearm. Riley looked at his left arm in agony as he tried to scream but nothing came out.

"Again!" Uncle D commanded.

I came down again on his left shoulder this time I heard a loud crunch on impact. His shrieking was haunting and everlasting. At this point I was hammering away at his biceps, wrists, hands, shoulders.

"Hold tight!" Focus shouted. "Come around the front now."

I swung the hammer at my feet while walking around the bench. Once I came to the front. I noticed his shoulders were dented unproportionally on both sides. His fingers were either broken or smashed up and his arms were purple and swollen like hot air balloons. He was drooling and his eyes were bloodshot red and rolling around in his head. They grabbed his legs and held them out straight then nodded for me to continue. As exhausted as I was, I found the will to raise the hammer once again for a series of brutal blows. His right knee shattered immediately with one strike. Then I worked on his upper thigh and waist until his pelvis was protruding from his flesh, but never broke the surface. I broke his shin backward with three good blows. Panting like an elephant in a relay, I found the strength to walk around the guys and started on his other leg.

When I finished with it, I took a knee with the hammer facing downwards and my right hand rested on top of it. The fellas laughed after they saw how tired I was. The squealing from Riley was fucking unbearable. It was like that newborn in the house at 4 am. He looked at me with the widest eyes I'd ever seen as if he was trying to speak to me with them. Staring back into them, I could see tears welling up and overflowing.

"Now his ribs Prince," Uncle D softly said.

I sucked a gust of air as I made it to my feet.

"No, Nooooo!!" he wept.

I had a batter's pose that would've put Babe Ruth' to shame.

CRACK! Blood shot out of his mouth like a dart and got on us all. He was clearly dying and I was glad for him.

I jumped over him and gave the other side my all as well. CRACK! There was a huge dent like crater on his right side. Finally, I sized his chest up and broke his sternum inward. Focus undid the straps and laid him on his stomach violently.

"Break his back!"

I hit him in the top of the back directly below the neck and demolished his spine. I beat him for about two minutes longer before they signaled for me to stop. I dropped the tool and fell out next to Riley. His body was purple and black. He was so swollen, he looked fake. He was wheezing like a wounded pig. Uncle D berated me.

"August, get the fuck up!"

"Uncle D, I'm dying too."

They laughed so hard, it pissed me off. "This nigga is done!" I said.

"Now you have to get rid of him, right?"

"Yeah."

"So pick him up and toss him across ya shoulder, then carry him to the hole," **Focus commanded.**

I looked at Focus like he was off his fucking meds or something. It took me a few minutes to gather my strength before I got him on my shoulder. He passed out from the pain, which was good for him. Other than being beaten half to death with a demolishing tool, no one wants to be buried alive. Uncle D went out ahead of us. After a short while, he returned to lead us out. Riley bled from his mouth and penis as I carried him along. He was probably 185 pounds, but it felt like 205 pounds. My shoulders and arms were on fire and shaking. I lunged forward with every step putting my all into it. Finally, I collapsed with him on top of me.

"Man down," Focus sarcastically stated.

"I'm good, give me a second."

"We have all night, Prince."

I pushed up and grabbed the tombstone in front of me and heard a whisper, **"Finish it lil man, I'm ready."**

We made it back up and started towards the plot.

"Never thought it would…be like this." Riley uttered.

I just listened as he rambled. Focus was a few feet behind us anyway.

"Lil man…I want you to know that…I will be waiting on you…"

"By the time I get there, you had better be a general in Lucifer's army, otherwise I'll conquer you in that life as well."

He chuckled slightly, "So, you know where you're going already huh…this righteous cause you kill for…. stand for…it will betray you in the end."

We arrived at the plot. Uncle D was leaning against a random tombstone nearby.

Focus said, "Cast him in and be done with it!"

"Lil man…along with you I'm taking a secret to my grave as well…do you know what it is?" Riley asked.

"What's that?"

"No matter how far you go…or how much success you have…you will eventually end up back where you started from…and that's right here with me."

"PRINCE!" Uncle D said, "That motherfucker is still alive! Damn he's resilient."

I threw him into the pit. He landed on his back facing upward. His eyes locked onto me with a gaze of sure promise that his words were already a part of me. The moonlight provided a mysterious gleam throughout the graveyard. I grabbed the shovel and positioned myself to cover the plot. I took a glance at my house and saw Thia standing at my window in her white garments. She watched everything as it happened. I knew then what her tears were for. My innocence was completely gone. After I buried him, Uncle D stood behind me and Focus stood in front.

"Stand on his grave, August." I followed Focus' instructions.

"Now take a knee."

As I kneeled into Riley's grave, Uncle D placed a silver dagger against my throat and a gun to the back of my head.

Focus was stern. "Prince, We bear witness to your capabilities under pressure, and we wholeheartedly respect your effort of transition within the family. The deed that you took part in has ridden the world of a man who profits off the downfall of the people. His success was obtained by tearing away at the foundation of our community, so you tore down the very fabric of his foundation in return. Now you kneel on his grave proclaiming yourself as a keeper of the balance. Our purpose is to enforce the barrier between the streets and civilians. When gangsters lose their way and oppress those who aren't involved in their world, we react. We don't protect rats or people who play both sides of the fence. We honor those with integrity who choose us over the police. When the community seeks refuge in us, it's because they want a special kind of justice or result. We must never move on anyone without a complaint or recommendation no matter what. Otherwise, the honor and class of our cause is lost. Anonymity is strongly encouraged for it conceals our identity as well as those we strive for. Karma doesn't always warrant death and during the course of your term, you will show versatility when honoring the requests made of the group. We are vigilantes who live above the law. We recognize that the government contributes to the problem and the solution can only come from within the people. The idea of physically overthrowing the ruler is possible, but not probable if you don't have the means to. Remember that Prince!

"Before you adopt our political agenda, you must first regulate anything within your reach. The Missing Tongue oath you took on the 28th was confirmation of your initiation into the Group. Tonight, the oath you will take is the "Sharp Tongue" which solidifies your allegiance to the Pack and its sovereignty. Let the moon bear witness as you repeat after me:

"If I should ever expose our way, Then I willingly become Karma's prey, Should I ever resist or attempt to flee, Then I forfeit the life which I have received, From moon to mountain, and earth to Ocean, I strive for Wisdom. Oath. Longevity. And fortune…My tongue is my sword!"

Uncle D followed up with, "This gun and dagger represent the wrath of your pack if you should ever violate or transgress. Your tongue will be cut from your head and the very thought of betrayal will be blown from its origin. Do you accept it?"

"Yes, I do!"

He lowered both weapons.

"Stand up Prince," Focus commanded!

"August, you are now the "Grey wolf" of the pack. You must display ambition, initiative, and an open mind to your elders. What happens in the pack stays in the pack! Never discuss our methods with Don or Thia. Our job is to uphold the balance and allow the moon to guide us into excellence. If you choose to pursue a career of any kind, we will support you. But make sure it benefits the group. This is an honor to see that you've adjusted to our ways. There will be prospects who are not of your bloodline, but they are not to be indoctrinated. Only your blood is worthy enough to bear the ring. We do not cooperate with government officials unless we mean to corrupt them to do our will. If you find yourself in interrogation, refer back to your oath of oral chastity. Your tongue should always be missing."

I nodded.

"Welcome to the balance," Uncle D added. "Just make sure your discipline restrains you from situations you must not indulge in, or you will involve your family. Focus and I have taken side contracts contrary to what we stand for and it never ends well so take my word for it."

"I understand Uncle D."

Do you have anything to say Prince?"

"Yeah, I promise to live up to everything that we stand for as a pack."

Focus and Uncle D just looked at each other in silence and gave a nod.

Chapter 16

Nell's family had gone to Jamaica for spring break, and we had been anticipating our next encounter since the incident with her father. They went twice a year, so she told them that she would go on the next one. I searched the house until I found the fellas in the backyard.

"Focus, I need to speak with you."

"What is it?" he replied.

"Could you drop me off at Nell's house?"

"Yeah, but what will you tell Thia?"

"That I'm with you."

"Oh really? Is that what you take me for?"

"C'mon Focus, I need you to do right by me on this please."

"Alright August, I got you, but you better be in some panties behind all of this deception."

Uncle D shook his head while saying, "Boy you a little horny motherfucker!"

They both laughed at me.

"What time are you tryna split?" Focus asked?

"I'm ready."

Alright, I will let Thia know, but you owe me Prince."

"I know and I will honor that when the time comes."

He nodded. I took off to call Nell to give her the news. Uncle D was pushing the Chevelle today, while Focus rode shotgun. The classic car was an extension of Focus' persona. The fact that he would let my Uncle drive said a lot.

"Listen up Prince," Uncle D commanded. "I heard about the incident with her father, and I would say he got off easy. He was in the right because you did invade his house, but he went about it the wrong way."

"Yeah, I feel you Uncle D."

"I know you and Nell are in love and shit so we will charge that mishap to the game. It needed to happen. That's why we are allowing you to go, because we know that she did her homework enough to call the right play."

I just nodded in silence.

"Alright nephew, enough with the bullshit; tell me the meaning of a wolf."

"We stand for wisdom, oath, longevity, and fortune."

"Good Prince, now let's elaborate on these attributes and why they make us who we are." Uncle D added, "Wisdom is accumulated philosophic or scientific learning, knowledge, also, insight."

"Good sense or good judgment." August stated before he continued.

Uncle D continued, "The more knowledge you gain, the better your understanding becomes towards all things. Wisdom sets in once you reach a broad level of understanding."

"Oath is a solemn appeal to God to witness to the truth of a statement or the sacredness of a promise. Your tongue is capable of bringing about life or death." August concluded.

"This is why you are sworn by two oaths which are one in the same. Uncle D "The missing tongue" is a promise to the group to never acknowledge our / its existence as a whole, while "The sharp tongue" reassures that your discretion be coerced or face retribution from the very ones you pledged to." Uncle D added. I continued:

"Longevity is a long life. No matter what happens you must remain durable as a man. Under no circumstances, shall another man or situation overcome you. We always find our way out.

"Finally, fortune is prosperity or a predetermined course of events often held to be an irresistible power or agency."

Focus interrupted, "It could also mean an abundance of wealth if you play your hand carefully. But don't be confused by material things at all, for the one who can outlast everyone else is always the most fortunate."

We pulled around to the back of the Nell's house. She was at the backdoor waiting for me. I jumped out and came around to Uncle D's window to give them a pound.

Focus said, "Tell her to come here."

I signaled for Nell to come over. She made her way without question. Once she got to the car, Focus apologized about that one thing and shook her hand. She accepted and shook Uncle D's hand as well. After she finished, we headed for the house while they pulled off and left us to it. The basement was the same. I came out of my sweatshirt exposing my physique to her.

"Look at you, August, with a fake buff ass." She gave me a big wet kiss on my lips. "Make yourself at home boy," she said as she handed me an ounce of weed and a box of blunts.

"Your lunch will be done in a little while ok."

I just nodded and started rolling up.

Her ass, hips, and thighs hugged her black pajama pants. She had a training bra on which exposed her shiny black skin. Her green bandana pushed her hair back into a ponytail. "Your curry chicken and rice are done," Nell shouted.

"Bring it down for me."

I turned the music down and finished the blunt. She returned with the plate and carrot juice. She sat Indian-style on the couch next to me and watched me eat. I changed the channel to CNN. After about a few minutes, she broke the silence in the room.

"There's something different about you, August."

"What do you mean girl?"

"Your whole demeanor is like…I don't know."

"Well, when you figure it out, let me know."

"I'm being serious, boo. Maybe it's because you haven't been over here in a while."

"I missed you too Nell." She grabbed me by my chin and kissed my greasy lips.

"Hurry up and finish so we can lay up boy!"

I didn't respond at all. I just continued to eat. Once I was done, she cleared the crime scene and jetted back to me.

I washed my hands and face in her bathroom, while she rolled up, of course. We laid up on the couch together. She put her head in my lap while I rubbed on her thighs. We were extremely mature for our age, but then again, I knew girls in the hood who had babies at 13 years old. Teenagers having sex became normal in Baltimore. We shared silence for a bit, enjoying each other's company. Nell and I were sky high beyond belief. Finally, we engaged in a conversation.

"August, are your people gangsters or something?"

"Not at all, why do you ask?"

"Well, I saw one of them in action already, and the other one looks tougher than him."

"They are just men of principle, Janell, that's all."

"I know their type August, but I hear you." She found herself on my lap passionately kissing me. She pulled back from me and smiled.

"You can have me today, August." I smiled as hard as any boy would've.

She got up from my lap and laid on her bed before signaled for me to come toward her. We finally had sex. I pulled out before I could make a mistake.

"Boy, you ain't shit." Nell snapped.

"Fuck you Nell, that shit feels too good to be lasting for hours."

She laughed and gave me a kiss before we got back into it.

The clock read half past 9 pm and the day had escaped us. I grabbed her cordless phone and called Focus to come get me.

I was heading out. I kissed her on her thigh without waking her then I snuck out the back door. The Chevelle was parked right outside the gate. I hopped over the fence and got into the passenger's seat. I gave Focus a pound and we were off.

"Prince, you smell like weed!"

"Yeah, I was smoking all day."

"Don't let Thia know or that's your ass! There's no need to ask about what happened because I can tell."

"Oh yeah, how is that?" I replied.

"You have a certain aura now about you. Just make sure that you respect the fact that she chose you to take her virginity. That's some sacred shit, August, and don't discard it."

When we got home, I dashed to the shower. Afterward, I made my way into my room and crashed.

Chapter 17

It was a scorching night in June. The east side ran red with the blood of the dealers in the game along with the tears of the mothers who raised them. The summer of '99 was ugly. Since Riley's disappearance, the streets were in an uproar and the pack kept me on ice until further notice. Don was scheduled to graduate next week, which was the only conversation Thia wanted to have. But tonight, she had something else on her mind. She said that we needed to be receptive to the message in class. I made the drinks as usual. Focus and Uncle D sat at the bar. Don and I sat on the couch and Thia relaxed in her Lay-Z-Boy with her book. Once everyone got settled, she opened up.

"It's good to see that our quest for knowledge has taken us to a level of conscious thought that seeks to remove the veils of illusion. Always remember that truth is all the same, but man tweaks it to make it look diverse. All paths should lead to self-realization (what you are at the core of your being) once you've awakened you can never go back to the unconscious masses."

I knew that this discussion would be one of those lessons that would reshape my perspective on life. She sipped her drink and began her lesson.

"These religions were designed to imprison the mind and engulf the emotions with fear and guilt. They were usually based on some savior figure and only by believing in them and following their dictates can we find God and be saved. That is precisely what the Babylonian priests said about Nimrod when the blueprint for control by religion was being molded in Babylon. To understand the true background of the religions we need to appreciate the basis of all ancient religions going back to the Phoenicians, the Babylonians, and beyond. It was the sun. The hierarchy focused on the sun because, as I outlined earlier, they understood its true power as an amazing generator of electromagnetic energy that has affected our lives and behavior every second of every day…the ancients took the circle of the zodiac and inserted a cross to mark the four seasons. At the center of the cross, is the sun. So many of the pre-Christian deities were said to have been born on December 25th because of this symbolism. On December 21st – 22nd you have the winter solstice. In the northern hemisphere, the sun is at the lowest point of its power in the annual cycle. The sun, the ancients said, had symbolically died. By December 25th the sun had begun its symbolic journey back to the summer and the peak of its power. The ancients, therefore, said that the sun was born on December 25th."

She closed the book and said, "That's a text from a book called "The Biggest Secret," by David Icke. Now boys, we believe through karma we create our blessings or misfortunes. As you can see, this whole belief system has been tampered with a great deal. Now we don't knock the people who practice the religions, but before you dedicate your life to something always cross reference to find its origins. Don't just follow something that you don't understand. God is already in you, my sons. The mind that you possess is a gift and it shouldn't be wasted on bullshit! All the answers to our questions are not outside of ourselves. We must punish our minds with education to sharpen our intellectual abilities. The fact that you have free will supports the reality of you having your life in your own hands." Don and I both nodded in agreement.

I lay in my bed that night reflecting on the group's message. I knew that letting go of my religious beliefs wouldn't happen overnight due to us being raised in the faith. But one thing I did know was that the truth never needed any support. Regardless of what, my family was the only thing real to me.

Chapter 18

The entire auditorium applauded in an uproar. Don was dressed in his blue cap and gown on the stage with the rest of the graduates. We were in the first row on the ground floor. Thia wanted a great view to see Don accept his award and give his small speech for the full scholarship he had earned. Uncle D was standing with the camcorder, while Focus, Thia, and I remained seated. After the principal gave his lengthy speech, it was time to give out the diplomas. We all stood up and clapped for Don when he received his diploma. Thia was crying along with Bella and Patti. My grandfather had a slight smirk on his face as he clapped and looked down at me.

"You're up next, aren't you?"

"Yes, sir," I replied

He put his arm around me and pulled me in close. Don grabbed his diploma with his left hand, then turned to us and held up his right fist. We all returned the gesture as a family.

We gathered at my grandparent's house for dinner. Ray sat at the head of the table, of course, and Patti was at the opposite end. My grandparents' house was home to us all. There was food everywhere. We all sat at the table for hours enjoying each other's company. Amid the good times, Thia announced to send Don and Neka to the Pocono's for the rest of the summer, paid in full. Things were good financially due to our extracurricular activities. Ray was sitting on the back patio to himself, as usual. I went outside to sit with him and catch up.

"What's going on granddaddy?"

"Hey there A, how's it going now?"

"Just taking it easy and taking notes from Don."

"Remember this buddy, people are placed in your life for you to learn from, good or bad. When you come across successful people, it's because they think of success and their words put you in a better place. But when you run

185

across a fool, the inspiration that you obtain from him is far better than anything else due to the fact that they show you how bad decision- making can destroy everything you've worked for."

That night, my brother and I sat on the back roof and smoked. We leveled with each other. "Don, why didn't you join the pack?"

"Because the family needs a financial advisor to balance things out. Don't get it twisted though August, I will kill if it comes down to it!"

"I didn't say you wouldn't Don."

"In time you will learn that everyone has their role to play and when I return from college, we will be able to expand our business legally. Just make sure you play your part and give these motherfuckers hell out here Prince!"

I looked at Don and smiled. He passed me the blunt and I focused my attention on Riley's grave.

"Don, are we going to hell?"

"August, what the fuck! No, we protect the people by all means. Our deeds put us in favor of good fortune. All you need to concern yourself with is the well-being of your family. There's only the higher self and lower self. Whichever you give into is your heaven or hell. Don't forget we are free from false doctrines of control. If you think that what you did to Riley was fucked up, then you have no idea how sinister the wolves really are, August."

"What do you mean?"

"Let's just say you have to be a certain kind of individual to run with them. I'm serious Prince, them motherfuckers are class A psychopaths. If it wasn't for the fraternity, they would be on death row somewhere. Just live well, August, and try your best to reach your true potential by working for it. Fuck Riley! He did dirt and got dirt in return. If we wouldn't have acted, there's no telling what he might've done!"

"I hear you Don"

"I needed to hear that bro."

As time went on, I did just that. A year had passed and Don was away at Penn State. The new millennium came hard. I spent the entire year training with the Pack. At 13 years old, I was ready to hunt properly. Focus made me a

marksman with various handguns, while Uncle D showed
me how to fuck people up, by of course, fucking me up first.

Chapter 19

My punches landed in flurries against his forearms. He taught me to breathe with every swing to preserve my energy. My left knee was in his chest applying pressure to his sternum. His arms were crossed-protecting his face and neck -- and I couldn't breach them. At will, he reached up and grabbed my neck with his right and stood up effortlessly putting my back to the ceiling. While he choked the hell out of me, his left fist was punching dents all over me. Luckily the weight training hardened my body enough to endure the punishment. I had managed to catch his arm with both hands and swung my knee upward into his chin. He finally released me. He shook it off and slowly approached me. There was an 80-pound harness strapped to me. We were fully engaged in combat before he began to narrate.

Uncle D grabbed my harness at the collar and slung me into the wall with great force. As I gained my balance, I reached out to grab his hands but instead, he gave me a power knee to the stomach. I threw up on him and collapsed to my knees. I felt his hands grip the waistband of my shorts as he elevated me into a spin cycle only to toss me across the room. I rolled violently and ended up in the push-up position. Drool was hanging from my mouth and my head was pounding. The harness fatigued me a great deal and made it hard to stand up. Focus was leaning up against a cement beam laughing and clapping his hands together.

Uncle D snapped at me, "Mercy is a luxury that you don't have, Prince, get up!"

He stood in a nonchalant pose and commanded me once again.

"You owe me two more minutes Prince, get the fuck up, and let's move!"

Climbing to my feet was like fighting gravity itself.

"He doesn't have anything left, Donavan," Focus stated.

I glared at Focus.

He threw his hands and said, "Don't hurt me, Prince!"

"That's all for now Prince, take a knee," Uncle D instructed.

"What a relief," Focus sarcastically stated.

The harness slammed to the floor when I peeled the Velcro straps off. I did the same with the shorts. We were in Mr. Phil's record shop's basement. There were no windows and it was soundproof. This is where we trained most of the time. It had also become our clubhouse since Phil brought Focus in as a silent partner. The weights migrated here, a full bar, big screen TV, couches, and a bed. Uncle D put a black rubber mat in the middle of the floor for us to spar on occasionally. The side door was our exit and entrance. After we got dressed, we headed home. When I got in, I ran upstairs to my room and found Thia sitting on my bed in the dark.

"What's up, Thia?"

"Sit down Prince, I have some news." Once I was seated, she hit me with it.

"August, Bella is sick. She has cancer and she is staying at Patti's right now."

"How long Thia?"

"The Dr. says six months give or take. Bottom line August, we are going to Patti's and contribute as a family, so get some rest, we leave in the morning."

After my shower, I fell back to wrap my head around a life without my dear Bella. She was everything to all of us. I knew she was old, but I had never lost anyone close before. Being strong was crucial right now because Thia barely held it together when she told me. I wondered how Don was going to take it.

The next morning, we arrived at Patti's. My grandmother cleared her room out and made it a hospice. Once Thia came out of her room, I went in, and Bella was sitting upright with her I.V. in her arm and the oxygen tank hooked around her face. She was alive and well and more than happy to see me.

"Get over here boy and give me a hug!"

She squeezed me tight and kissed me on my face over and over. I sat next to her as we conversed.

"How's school love?"

"Fine Bella, I'm going to high school in September."

"Where does the time go, August? we are all very proud of you."

"Bella, what's wrong with you?"

She paused and said, "I'm leaving baby."

"Why?"

"Well August, when you've served your purpose in life and you live as long as I did, no matter how strong your spirit is, eventually your body gets weak. Truthfully, I don't fear death at all because God lives in me and He's everlasting, so my soul shall live with Him forever. Don't cry for me August, you need to rejoice when someone goes home and cries when a baby is born into this treacherous world. When I go August, and I will go, make sure that no matter what life brings you, whether evil or righteous, use it

193

as a stepping stone to reach your true potential in life. When you become a man, you will have to protect the family. Promise me August, that you will stand with family and honor God above all else because He is yours."

"I promise Bella."

She went silent and turned her attention to the window. The sun was gleaming through into the room like God was stopping by to check on his homegirl. I stared into the light along with her.

Bella died peacefully in her sleep two weeks later. The fucking doctor gave her six months, but it took her within three weeks. Her funeral was on a Tuesday the following week. Don made his way down, of course. Everyone was dressed to the nine but me. The pain of losing Bella was so deep, I just could not bring myself to go. I stayed in the room Bella died in for most of the day. I couldn't cry for the fact that Bella told me not to. I had mixed emotions about this life and the next. Over the next few months, I used the hunt to suppress my emotions.

***

Focus made a left onto Ashland and walked in the target's direction. His house was three doors from the corner.

"Tiffany, who the fuck is this walking down here?" The man said as Focus drew closer.

She replied, "I don't know, I ain't never seen him before."

The man got off the steps and started towards the corner. Focus whistled loudly. Uncle D said, "The target is on the move Prince, it might be a chase."

I rushed to the corner next to Uncle D. We both watched as he came under the streetlight on the corner and started towards the cars on our side. Before he could get to whatever he was going for, Focus darted around the corner at full speed towards him. Without a chance to think, he just took off. He ran across the street and into the alley on the other side.

Focus ran directly past us and said, "I-ma get the car ready!"

Uncle D commanded, "Get him Prince!"

I took off behind him and got on his ass. We chased him down Ashland and made a right onto Linwood towards Madison. I caught Rock as he mounted the curve on the left side of Linwood. I reached out and grabbed his white T and slung him into the brick wall on the side of the corner house.

"Move Prince!" Uncle D shouted.

As I stepped out of the way, Uncle D picked Rock up off the ground and slammed him straight onto his head knocking him out cold.

"Oh my God!" A girl shouted from her window from across the street.

I unzipped my pocket and pulled out the razor. I rolled him over and put my knee in his throat. "Hurry up Prince!"

I stuffed my hand into his mouth and gripped his tongue. Once I had it fully extended, I sliced his shit off! The blood squirted out of his face and onto my shirt.

"What the fuck!" She shouted again. Uncle D snatched me up.

"C'mon!"

We bailed back up Linwood, made a left on Ashland Avenue then made a right on Kenwood. People were out on their porches watching us tear through their block like a relay. Suddenly three shots went off! Boom, Boom, Boom!

"Hit the alley, Prince!"

We both darted left into the alley and made a sharp right up the middle of the alley towards Eager Street. Uncle D and I scanned every yard on our way up. Once we got to Eager, we walked to Focus' car and got in. He pulled off slowly and made the first right onto Lakewood, then took it straight up.

"So, did the Prince come through or what?"

Uncle D replied, "The kid's a natural brother. August, why don't you show him?"

I held Rock's tongue over the seat covered in blood. Focus glanced at it through the rear-view and said, "Would you look at that, we have ourselves a gray, Donavan."

"It's in his blood," Uncle D replied.

I sat back and looked out the window while we made a left onto Biddle Street and then a right on Milton Avenue.

Half the houses were vacant and boarded up. We made a right on Hoffman Street and passed JJ's for a few blocks before we stopped.

"Here we are Prince," Uncle D stated. The block was clear and I didn't see a soul. The clock read 2:20 am. Uncle D began to instruct me on this last target.

So far, you've done very well Prince and our respect was yours back when you killed Riley. Now understand when I say that we are not turning you into a killer…no, that shit is already in you Prince. What we're transforming you into is something political, something intellectual, something tangible, something other than anything else that derives from the pits of East Baltimore or any other ghetto in this world. This is the way you have to be and this is the way that you must think. We must kill any and everybody who destroys our people and at this moment, we are only operating within our means. You and Don will place us in positions where we can be effective."

He passed me a black 32-automatic handgun and said, "Do you see that black Grand Cherokee parked four doors down?"

"Yeah, I see it."

"The target owns that car, and when he goes to get in his car, you will take his life from him."

"That's not a problem Uncle D."

"Good, he leaves for work within the hour so brace yourself."

Focus added, "Now when you clap someone, you don't "shoot 'em up" Prince. You be precise, always hit them in the chest first; this folds your victim up and when he hits the ground, he will ball up leaving his head vulnerable.

I just nodded in agreement.

"Good, now go. I will spin the car around and park at the top of the block."

I got out of the car and shut the door. Uncle D rolled his window down and said, "Lay yourself underneath his truck so you remain unseen."

I nodded and started down Mura Street. I climbed under the truck and got comfortable.

"I love my baby cousin," Focus said.

Cars were riding down the block one after another. I laid on my stomach for about an hour. My adrenaline was surging throughout my body like electricity. I heard a door open up behind me on the left. I turned back as far as I could to get a visual. Once the screen door slammed shut, I heard a horn honk one time. Common sense told me that it was the signal. The man mounted the sidewalk and headed towards me. The car alarm was deactivated, and the front headlights flashed. *Yeah, this is him,* I thought. As he drew closer to the truck, I crawled carefully from under the passenger's side until I was out. I crept around the front of the car in between the rear of another and waited for him to open his door. Once I heard the keys, I got set. When the driver's door opened up, I jumped straight into action, coming from around the car quickly. He had one leg in the car which gave me the advantage. I rushed him pushing the door shut. His neck was wedged in the corner of the door causing him to choke. I leaned in to put all my weight on the door before he reached his left hand out to punch me. He began to push the door slightly off him. Once both of his hands were placed on the door, I raised the pistol with my right hand and shot him through his left eye. I released the door and he fell into the gutter on his face. I didn't see an exit wound, so I kneeled and shot him in the back of his head. I froze up after I saw the blood fill the gutter underneath him. A voice took me out of the trance.

"Prince!"

I looked up and Uncle D was standing at the corner on the opposite side. I ran towards him, and we both got in the car. Focus took off.

Uncle D stated, "We don't do that Prince! Don't ever freeze up homie, you got it!"

"Yeah, it was just…"

"I know," he interrupted. "Don't worry about it, it's done."

We hit Federal and Lakewood in no time. Focus drove straight across the street towards the junkyard. Uncle D and I got out and walked down the alley while Focus made a U-turn and drove off. It was hot outside already, and the sun wasn't even up yet. We made it into the house and went down into the basement. I went in the back, stripped my clothes off, and jumped in the shower. I watched as the blood ran down the drain and I remember feeling invincible beyond all else. The reality of me contributing to our cause gave me a newfound respect for myself. And the people who mattered the most to me in life knew that I was committed to the agenda and its progress.

When I got out of the shower, my clothes were gone, and my shorts were lying on the bed. I put them on and went up front. Uncle D was sitting at the bar with an empty glass in his hand. I walked behind the bar and grabbed the glass from him then cleaned it with the bar towel. Afterward, I poured him a nice shot of Remi Martin. He raised his glass to me and took a sip. When he lowered it, he spoke to me.

"Prince, your work tonight was outstanding besides that little episode at the end."

I nodded as he went on.

"Our thoughts reflect our actions, and our deeds determine who we are. Let me tell you the difference between *karma and prey*; now karma is personal requests from the people. Usually, these targets are disrespectful or exploit the hardships of the community. Therefore, we step in and act as retribution on behalf of the civilians who cannot defend themselves. Take Rock for instance. He thought it was cool to speak on things that didn't concern him while employing his facts and breeding controversy. He also managed to get a few guys shot, which brought the police into the neighborhood. And you know we don't want that, because with them comes harassment and some brutality. Now prey is exactly what it is, Prince. These are the motherfuckers that are beyond saving and they play the game too raw. They kill homeboys, cooperate with the law, corrupt the children, rape the women, etc. These people make our conditions much harder. They take everything out of the hood and don't give shit back. They are a brand of oppressors who are far worse than the government because they know our weaknesses and they would be the ones to sell us out."

"I hear you Uncle D, but we are killing our own nonetheless."

"Indeed, Prince, but the key to change is to rebuild from the inside out and you must keep that in mind. Only we can help ourselves, August."

"I have a question."

"What's that?"

"How do you know where these targets are all the time or where they will be?"

"It's simple, the community provides a location for us. That nosey-ass neighbor who always sits in the window, she's with us all the way. We have eyes all over the place Prince, don't trip."

"That's cool but what happens when they give us up?"

"We have that covered too. We have a government official who will inform us of any heat. They also clear the street for us while we hunt."

"Damn Uncle D!"

"Yeah, Prince, I hope you didn't think that we were just that damn good."

"I did."

"However, things will not always run smooth Prince and there will be a worthy adversary sooner or later. But you never know your true strength, until you run across a real foe."

"So, we are vigilantes then?"

"Without a doubt, if you look at it from their point of view. But we are more so revolutionaries who choose not to protest and bitch about our conditions. We do something about it. But you, August, are more than that. You and Don will launch a campaign that's going to even the playing field completely. My nephews are not revolutionaries but the first breed of Evolutionaries."

Chapter 20

Coming through the hallways was just like Don told me it would be. The guys were tougher and divided into their cliques. They all wore their flight jackets with their hoods stitched on the back of them. The girls were overly developed in all forms. This was high school. I had never seen this much breast and ass in one place. The west side was its civilization. I was two weeks in at North-Western High on Park Heights. My subject was still language arts and history. Everything else could fuck off! Lunchtime was like recess. Park Heights was known for dope and death, but little did they know, I was a dope boy killer. By this time, I was well into the hunt with my pack. My folks were well off, and I kept money to buy my usual primetime pizza, butter crunch cookies, and a kiwi strawberry Snapple every day for lunch. We wore uniforms in high school as well. However, West Baltimore was a fashion show and everybody had the latest of everything. Trying to keep up with these niggas would've got me robbed on the Eastside. Plus, I learned a long time ago to never show my wealth. After I ate, I took off to roam the halls until 3rd period. I fell into a routine of hanging on the 3rd-floor stairway talking to Ms. Larue on my cell phone. Our relationship had grown a great deal and she still made time to tutor me as well. I took a seat on the steps and hit her phone.

She answered, "Hey August."

"What's up, Ms. L?"

"I'm in the teacher's lounge right now and I figured that you would call, so I kept my phone out. So how is high school?"

"It's cool but there's a lot of distractions if you know what I mean."

"What is it? Too much ass for you August?"

"Not at all Ms. L, but it's just so available, you know."

"Um hmm, don't make me come up there, boy! I remember you and Janell's fast ass in the stairwell."

"Ms. L, I'm focused enough to stay on point, plus Nell and I are still a factor."

"Yeah, but Janell is at Mergenthaler High School in Northeast Baltimore and there's no telling what she's doing!"

"Anyways, when can we link up?"

"Well, how about I pick you up after school on Friday and we hang out?"

"That's cool, so I will see you then?"

"Take care August."

I made my way down the stairs and ran into a dice game. It had to be about a dozen motherfuckers packed in the stairway, smoking weed, and listening to their CD players.

"Who the fuck are you?" Someone unfamiliar shouted out.

Once I heard that I immediately tried to avoid the situation. "Fellas I'm just tryna get past, that's all."

The so-called leader spoke up, "I don't give a fuck, go around the other way!"

I figured it was now or never to put the east side in these niggas' life. I lunged off the steps and punched the leader knowing that I was in for an ass whippin'. I pushed him up against the wall and they all swarmed me. There were so many of them that I couldn't feel anything. So, I just went in on the one I had a hold of. They tried to get me on the ground, but I didn't go for it. After a while, I heard arguing between them and some other guys. They jumped off me and started fighting some other gang. At this time, the leader and I were still engaged until I felt a fist crack me from behind sending me up against the wall. When I shook it off, I tried to slide off down the steps, but it was too chaotic. The leader had two niggas on his ass so I just helped him out, fuck it. I grabbed one of them from behind by his collar and wrapped my hand around it, then started working on him. I had no clue why we were scrapping but this looked like some gang shit. I remember thinking, *where the fuck is the school police at?* Shit hit the fan like I had never seen. One of the guys yelled, "Timeout!"

Everybody started to scatter like roaches, and I followed the crowd. We ran back up the steps and into the hall. We tore through the halls like a track meet until we made it to a crowd. I blended in and walked down to the 2nd floor straight to my locker. Once I grabbed my books, I went to class and took a seat. Now as I've told you before, math wasn't my favorite, but I was happy to be in that bitch that day. I participated and everything. When we changed classes, I kept my head down and took it straight to social studies. Now I was no coward by far, but my folks didn't play that fucking up in school shit. So, I tried to respect their wishes and avoid the drama. Thia sent me over here because I didn't know anybody and for safety purposes. She wanted me away from the east side when I went to school, and I understood that fully. About a half hour into class, I felt a tap on my right shoulder. I turned and saw a light-brown-skinned hazel-eyed girl. She had skinny single braids on her head and she was thick.

She said, "You have a cut behind your ear and on your neck."

"Oh yeah," I replied,

"Um hmm, it looks like scratches. Here…" She handed me her small mirror to check it out.

"No thanks, I trust your word baby."

She smiled, snapped her neck back, and said, "I'm not your baby, my name is Renae!"

"My name is August. Can you clean this up for me?"

"What would your girlfriend think about that?"

"My girl is across the fucking planet somewhere."

"So that's how you get down? Trying to holla at me when you have a girl?" I just looked at her while she shook her head and got back to work. I played it off because she pulled my card. I knew that she was on me, and it was only a matter of time before we spoke again.

Class let out and I caught Renae at her locker.

"So, can you help me with my paper cuts?"

Renae turned to look at me and shifted her weight to poke her ass out.

"Boy, you don't want anything!"

"Patch me up girl, I know you got something in there."

"Come here and lean over." I leaned into her and she cleaned my scratches with some alcohol pads from the nursing program.

"Thank you so much."

"Boy shut the fuck up you just chasing for real!"

"Why do you keep talking to me like that girl?"

"Because niggas only want one thing."

"Look, I'm not these niggas and I'm not what you're used to either. I don't know anybody over here so I figured you would be the one to show me this side of town."

"Nigga, please! You are trying to break me in with that weak-ass game of yours boy!"

I couldn't help but laugh at her. She was on to me. She laughed, shut her locker, and walked off. When I got outside, Uncle D was eating his club sandwich on the hood of his caddy in the parking lot across the street. I gave him a pound and jumped in the passenger's seat. When we hit Northern Parkway, he conversed with me.

"So was sup Prince?"

"Nothing much, I got a lotta homework and shit."

"Good, the more you know then."

"I guess so, where's Focus?"

"He's laid up with Tammy down on Orleans and Colington. Your mother is down the house with your Aunt Wanda and Stacey talking shit." My phone vibrated and when I checked, it was Nell.

"Wus up girl."

"Hey baby can I see you? I need a sample."

"Ard girl hold on." I covered the phone. "Uncle D, can you drop me off at Nell's?"

"Yeah, I got you."

I was happy to report to Nell, "I'm on my way, boo."

We hung up and we shot over to Nell's. Uncle D still covered for me, plus he had to get laid himself. Nell was giving me a massage after I finished my homework. Eventually, it led to sex as usual. We smoked right after and talked for a minute before I called a sedan and made my way home around 7 pm. My curfew was 9, but I didn't play in the street too much due to my position in the fraternity. I had the sedan drop me off on Rose Street, and I walked the rest of the way. My stroll up the dark alley always gave me a reality check of my environment. The rats didn't acknowledge me at all while they excavated each trash can. When I got into the backyard, I could hear the girls talking from the living room. I walked through the backdoor and locked it behind me.

"There he is," Thia said.

As I walked through the dining room towards the living room everything was polished. From the floors, baseboards, and tables, down to our pictures. My mother was truly a maniac for neatness.

"Wus up A!" Stacey shouted.

"School and these hoes" I replied. I felt my mother breaking her glaring at me while everyone else laughed. Aunt Wanda put her two cents in.

"August, don't make Thia fuck you and them hoes up boy!"

I quickly gave them all kisses on their cheeks and stood against the wall in between the hallway and the living room.

"So how is high school lil nigga?"

Once Aunt Wanda made that statement, I knew that it wasn't juice in their glasses.

I responded, "I'm just taking it one day at a time, you know. Trying to conform to their style of academics."

"Ooow, conform huh? Did you hear that, Stacey?"

"Yeah, I heard him on his "conforming shit!"

Thia interrupted them, "You two bitches are drunk! That is a common word."

We all laughed. Thia asked, "I know I don't have to ask you about homework, do I?"

"Nope, I did it in class, but you can check it."

"No, I trust your word until proven otherwise. How did you get home?"

"Uncle D dropped me off and went about his business."

"Yeah, he told me y'all were hanging out after school." I nodded, trying not to say too much. She studied me for a minute and simply said, "OK."

I gave everyone a salute and took it upstairs. Shortly after my shower, I settled in my room on the phone with Nell.

"Damn August, you nailed me, boy."

"Well, that's what you told me to do right?"

"Yes, but it's like you're getting better and better every time. You not fucking other bitches, are you?"

"Nell, I don't have the time to do all that, on some real shit."

"Good because I will kill a bitch to death about you!"

"Slow down girl, remember it takes two to tango."

"Right, and your ass will get it too!"

I laughed as usual and got a call on my cell from Ms. Larue. I let it vibrate, then texted her back, "Give me 5 minutes."

She texted back, "1 minute."

"Alright, Nell, I'm ready to go eat, let me hit you back in a few."

"I love you August."

"I love you more Nell, later."

While we were hanging up, I was dialing Ms. L. She picked up.

"Hmm, so what were you doing that you had to put me on the back burner?"

"I was talking to my girl."

"I figured as much."

"So, are we still on for Friday?"

"That's what I said, and we will be discussing The Harlem Renaissance while we eat."

"Cool." I simply replied.

"August, your level of comprehension is very high, and I love you like a son. But the number of homicides in your area scares the shit out of me baby. The mentality that you have, it would be such a waste if you were to fall victim to the bullshit, you feel me?"

"Yeah, I feel you Ms. L, but it's minds like mine that can benefit my neighborhood. Change has to come from within first. You see, all everyone else can go off of is what they put in the media. They control our image, which molds an outsider's perception. But there are good people down here who stand for each other. The conditions breed despair to the point where struggle becomes the norm."

"I'm with you August but don't you want to see the world eventually?"

"Doesn't everyone, Ms. L? But trust my words when I say that if you turn your back on a problem that you have the means to be the solution to, then you might as well choose your place amongst the conquered who succumb to their demise."

"Damn boy! I had no idea that you felt so passionate about the people."

"Why do you think I study so hard Ms. L?"

"I get it, August, and I will continue to help you anyway that I can, that's my word."

"And at the end of the day, Ms. L, that's all I can ask for."

***

Friday afternoon I was in class anticipating my date with Ms. L. Renae who was flirting all day long, but it was nothing serious. I got up to use the bathroom only to kill time. I was planning to just hang in there for about five or ten minutes. Shortly after, two guys walked in to do the same. At first, I didn't pay them any attention, but they knew me.

"A yo!" One of them said I looked up at him.

"You were beefing with us on the stairway the other day, weren't you?"

"Are you asking me or telling me?" I replied sharply.

"It doesn't matter, we getting ready to fuck you up anyway because we don't fuck with up top niggas."

I replied, "Look I don't give a fuck about no up top, underneath, or none of that. I'm from over east my nigga!"

They looked at each other and he responded, "Oh, we don't fuck with no east side niggas at all."

I took my shirt off and threw it in his face, then I went at his man. They jumped me of course, but not like they wanted to. Uncle D taught me how to keep two people off of me and my strength just enhanced everything. I ended up on the opposite side of the bathroom by the door while both of them were breathing heavily at the window. My white beater was torn and bloodied. I ripped it off and wet it enough to wipe my lip. Then I swiped my uniform shirt off the floor and left. On my way back to class, I was pissed off but satisfied at the same time. Before I got to class, I tossed my tank top in the locker.

When I sat down, I turned to Renae and said, "Do you have something for this?"

"Boy, you stay getting trashed around this motherfucker! Let me see it, August!"

She grabbed my face and pulled me in to examine it.

"How is it?"

"It's not bad at all punk!" As she let my face go, I kissed her hand.

She responded quickly, "That's why I just changed my pad with that hand!"

"Girl what the fuck!"

"Sike boy, but don't do that -- you got a girl remember?"

She giggled and rubbed me on my back. When I got outside, I started up the street towards Reisterstown Road to meet Ms. L at the Dunkin Donuts. But during my travels, I spotted Renae putting her books in the trunk of a car on one of the side streets. This was a fine time to press up, so came the detour. As she put the key in the front door she said, "I see you August!"

"Girl, I just wanted to wish you well for the weekend."

"Bullshit!"

"Renae, why do you keep shooting me down all the time?"

"Because I'm up to you niggas out here. All you want to do is fuck me or use me for what I can do for you, plus you got a girl August!"

"Check this out Nae, I don't want shit from you because I don't know what you have. And I won't lie, sex has crossed my mind, but the more we talk, the more I respect you. I do have a girl and I've been dealing with her for a minute. All I want is to catch you away from school here and there and find out who you are as a person."

"You can find all that right here boy, what's the difference?"

I had her, all I had to do was keep talking, but the drama didn't quit.

"A yo!"

I turned around to a mob of niggas. It was the leader that I punched the other day. I instructed Renae to get into her car and she did. They all had free-size t-shirts on with fitted hats.

"Let me holla at you."

We approached each other and he said, "My nigga good lookin' out on that one shit a few days ago. As far as me and you, I'll let that go if you will."

I nodded in relief and gave him a five, thankful that I didn't get trashed in front of my future piece. They strolled off and I leaned on Renae's window to engage her once again.

"Boy, I thought that you were from the east side?"

"I am."

"Well, how do you Dime?"

"I don't."

"Whatever August don't get caught up, they're at war with them down bottom niggas." So, Dime is from up top?" I asked.

"Yeah, and they can't stand each other for shit."

"So where are you from Renae?"

"Walbrook Junction, but I live on Oakfield Ave and Springdale right now."

"Tell you what girl -- take my number and hit me when you are ready."

She gave me her phone and I programmed it in. She pulled off and I shot up the street. When I got to the donut shop, Ms. L was parked in the lot. I jumped into the front seat and placed books on the backseat behind us.

"Where's my hug boy?"

We leaned in and hugged, then I kissed her on her right cheek. She smelled like apples and cinnamon. She had those fish-scaled French braids going upward in her head. I swore she was my girl, too.

We stopped in Eastpoint and got something to eat. When we got our food, we started to catch up.

"I haven't seen you in about a month, August, what's been up?"

"Just helping my folks sort out issues within the family."

"Have you been holding strong since Bella passed?"

"Yeah, and I think about her a lot, that's why I cherish people because you never know."

"That's right baby, your heart is in the right place and your mind state is in an even better position. Since you were younger August, you've always had a good sense of understanding when it comes to life. The things that you study don't strike the interests of other kids."

Bitch I ain't no kid is what I thought to myself.

"So, put me down with the Harlem Renaissance."

"Well, African American writers migrated from the South seeking opportunity in the cities up north. In 1903, W.E.B DuBois contributed a controversial landmark book called "The Souls of Black Folk about life and opportunity for African Americans in the United States." By the 1920s, Harlem had become a mecca for men and women of color. Langston Hughes (1902-1967) was one of many to flourish in Harlem along with Nella Larsen, Zora Neale Hurston, Claude McKay, etc. Do you know why I chose to discuss this topic of history?"

"Why Ms. L?"

"Because it's a prime example of how people seek out a better life in places of opportunity. These individuals knew that the environment they came from was unproductive and had no outlet for them to explore their true potential."

"Are we talking about my neighborhood Ms. L?"

She shrugged her shoulders as if saying *if the shoe fits...*

"All I'm saying, August is that you should begin to consider every option that is available to you outside of Baltimore. Sometimes people have to relocate to see what life truly has to offer."

"I feel you Ms. Larue and I will travel in the future."

"So, what is it about your neighborhood that has your attention so much?"

I made sure to choose my words wisely. "Ms. Larue, people are constantly leaving Baltimore once they get situated financially. Now this isn't a bad thing at all, it's their life and they have to do what's best for them and their families regardless. But it's the staying away part that pisses me off, you know. If you have the means to rebuild and make a small change, then why not?"

"Maybe it's because they want better for their children, August."

"But what about the good people who can't make it out and want the same thing?"

She had no response, so I went on.

"The reason every ghetto around the world is suffering the same fate is because the kids have nothing to look forward to. When the city tears down the rec centers, puts a liquor store on every corner, and tells you that you can't hang with your friends on a block that y'all were born and raised on, how fair do you think that is?"

"C'mon now August. I watch the news and I see what goes on down there."

"Ms. L, I'm not saying that we don't contribute to the problem, because we do. Most of the destruction derives from the drug epidemic that strings the parents out and leaves a ten-year-old to take care of his or her younger siblings. Drug dealers are made by poverty and ignorance mixed with pressure. I have yet to meet a dope boy that came from money and if so, he's from one of those Mexican or Colombian cartels or something. Half the niggas down their hustle for a better life. They don't want to be there Ms. L no matter how slick we try to make it look. We know that there's something better out there."

"As I said before boy, you are very passionate when it comes to your people, and I guess nothing can change your mind about them."

"It's not about changing my mind Ms. L, just show me better ways to be productive. I want you to mold me with all the tools that you are working with."

"Oh, believe me, August, I'm all over that."

I was all over that innuendo she just threw me too, in case she didn't think I caught it. I was horny on the regular and the possibility of me nailing a grown woman as bad as she put my confidence at an all-time high.

She interrupted my thoughts stating, "Life has a way of working out harsh conditions and making way for the next obstacle. Something tells me that you will play a part in its process of transition. Am I right?"

I locked eyes with her and replied, "Ms. Larue, you haven't the slightest idea."

Chapter 21

"Witnesses are saying that the suspect had on a dark-colored sweatsuit, a bandana, a hat, and black tennis shoes.

"I'm Bob Blake reporting live from Steeper and Monument Streets in East Baltimore where we have yet another heinous murder. The witness chose to remain anonymous as they gave this statement. I was sitting on my porch and the guy pulled up in his truck and got out about two doors down to see his family. He was standing on the curb for a few minutes when this guy came out of Steeper Street at full speed. He shot him in the chest and grabbed him by his shirt. All in one motion, he slung him around and the guy went straight into traffic. I have never seen anything like it and whoever the boy is that did it, should be off the streets immediately! I heard cars screeching as they slammed on their brakes and then I heard a loud Boom! To tell you the truth, I covered my eyes and looked away. When I looked back up, the guy was lying in the street on his back and the suspect was gone without a trace. I've been living here for over 15 years, and I've seen it all. But now these kids are finding new ways to kill each other. It's time for me and mine to go!

"This has been Bob Blake reporting from East Baltimore. Police are asking for help from the community. The suspect is 5 '5 and had on a dark-colored sweat suit; if you know this person, please call the number at the bottom of your screen."

Thia muted the TV and looked at me while shaking her head.

"Too brazen!" she shouted. "Now I don't orchestrate the hunt and I won't infringe on the pack at all, but your little ass is zapping out! Are you having fun, August?"

I just sat there shifting my weight. She pointed at the TV. "Look at this shit! People are not ready for this at all."

I replied, "So, what do you suggest?"

She watched me for a while before she sighed and said, "Just be careful baby boy, alright."

"Yes, ma'am I will."

She set the remote on the table, got up, and kissed me on my forehead then went up the steps. Once we heard her room door slam Uncle D said, "Prince don't mind her, she's just in shock at how ruthless you've become. They don't have anything on you, just an outfit and height. Half of the dudes running around town are short as a motherfucker!"

Focus came into the living room from the kitchen eating his sandwich. He stood in front of us both and said, "We got to make our way across the street to meet the pig."

He threw me the keys. "Prince, go tighten the place up while I speak to your uncle. We'll meet you over there in a minute."

I opened the master lock and pulled it off, then slid both latches up and opened the side door to Phil's. I shut it behind me and started down the steps. It was pitch black throughout the entire basement. I hit the switch at the bottom of the steps and grabbed the push broom in one motion. My job was to make the den, as we called it, presentable for the meeting. I put the weights back onto the rack, rolled the mat up against the wall, and stood it up. Then I swept the rug between the couches after I beat it half to death. After that, I swept the entire basement and I wiped down the bar, couches, mirrors, and TV. Believe it or not, I loved cleaning more than anything else thanks to my mother. Once all the trash was gathered and tied up in the bag. I threw it over my shoulder to take it out. When I opened the side door and stepped out, Focus and Uncle D were just making it across the street towards me.

"Everything's in order," I said. "This trash is the last of it."

Focus responded, "Hurry up and come back inside."

He went in while Uncle D stood beside me as I put the bag into the trash can.

"Prince, we want you to stick around and listen carefully. You've proven yourself enough to know how strong the pack's aim is on the low." He put his arm around me and guided me back into the basement shutting the door behind him. Focus was sitting with his feet on the coffee table watching TV.

Uncle D said, "Damn, this bitch is spotless, August!"

"Good job," Focus added. As we took our seats.

I remember thinking they never let me meet the pig and to sit in on a meeting like this meant that I was highly respected by the wolves. Uncle D and I played a few games of chess before Focus' phone went off. He got up and said, "He's here. I'll let him in Prince -- you go behind the bar and prepare our drinks, will you?"

As I shot behind the bar to clean the glasses, Focus went up the steps and out of the door. Uncle D sat back onto the couch and crossed his legs stating,

"Believe it or not August, the Pig wants to meet you himself."

"Why?"

"Well, why not let your talent speak for itself?"

"Who is he supposed to be Uncle?"

He just smiled and requested Remi on the rocks. While their drinks were being prepared, Focus slammed the door shut and came back down with another guy. He was tall with a muscular build and a lighter skin tone.

"What are you drinking?" I asked the new guy.

He looked in my direction and said, "Is this the Prince?"

"Yeah, that's me, who are you?"

Focus put his hands on the guy's shoulder and guided him over to the couches before he looked back and said Remi with no ice. I brought all three drinks over to the table and set them down. I couldn't help but notice the guy was staring at me the entire time. When I went back behind the bar to clean up, Focus instructed me to come have a seat and bring the bottle as well. I took a seat next to Uncle D across from the new guy so I could see him. It was about 1 am. The guy pulled out an ounce of weed from his leather jacket and threw it on the table.

"Who is that for?" I asked.

They all laughed and said, "Not us!"

The guy stated, "I brought that for you Prince."

I replied, "Well you're off to a good start with me!"

He laughed a little and said, "I heard, so there you go."

"Why are you doing this? I don't know you." I asked.

"Yes, you do," he replied.

"From where then?"

"I was there when Althia had you at Johns Hopkins back in 87."

"Oh yeah?"

"That's right and now you're the gray wolf and shit!"

I looked at Focus and Uncle to find them watching me carefully. The guy recited the missing tongue oath word for word as I turned my attention back to him. He had to be family to know about the fraternity.

"This is my little brother," Focus said. "He's your cousin Pig."

"Why do we call him Pig?"

Uncle D said, "Because he was a fat fuck growing up, ain't that right Fran-Fran."

"Don't call me that, Donavan. I hate that. Prince, my name is Francis, but you can call me Pig."

I got up and embraced him with a hug and he kissed me on my head. When I sat down, I rolled up automatically when I saw that he had blunts too. He said, "Everybody in the division is talking about you, Prince."

"What do you mean division?"

He pulled his badge out and said, "My boys!"

"You're a cop?" I snarled.

"Hell yeah."

"How do you think the pack can do what y'all do without a chase? I'm the one that clears the police out of the area when y'all hunt. Look at me as the house nigga giving the field niggas intel."

I nodded and lit the blunt.

"Alright Pig, tell us something," Focus interrupted.

Pig started in. "Fellas I have some info on a shipment of guns coming in from VA in 3 hours."

"Damn pig, that's short notice!" Uncle D said.

"I know but my source just put me down. So, I figured that I would call in a favor from the wolves to interrupt the shipment and ice these dirty badges in the process."

"They're some of yours?" Uncle D asked.

"They work at the western district on the gun task squad. Word is the guns are going to Curtis Bay in South Baltimore."

"Where's the checkpoint for us to strike where the shipment is going to be?" Focus asked.

"Bryant Avenue at the high-rise apartments. Whitelock is hot as shit, but that area is quiet enough to get it done. All we have to do is create a small diversion and send my boys in the opposite direction. I have no jurisdiction over there so we will have to make a window to get it done."

"So, what are the terms if we help you and your so-called source?" Focus asked.

"Well, we get to keep these guns off the streets and out of the hands of kids. The wolves can keep a third of the arsenal for themselves for future activities; there's five grand a piece in it for you as well. Most of all, it would be wise to make good on my word to my source, who could help me to power later on."

"This shit is an illegal Pig! So, your source must be a crook as well," Uncle D snapped.

"Listen, fellas, when I took my vow to this group, I meant it. And with that said, we must do what's needed to further our agenda by all means. One day, I will be the fucking commissioner or the mayor even and then we will be untouchable. I'm just asking the pack to trust me and continue to be the keepers of the balance." I put my blunt out a long time ago because this shit was heavy.

"Alright!" Focus said. "We will help, but the Prince isn't ready for this."

"Yes, I am! My oath is just as valid as anybody else in this den!"

"I didn't say you weren't going Prince because we need you. I'm saying that you will create the diversion while we hijack the shipment. One thing I know about cartel cops is that they are hired guns as well and you never had anyone shoot back at you yet, now have you?"

"No, I haven't."

"Pig, what did you have in mind as far as how the diversion should go?"

"Well, there are more ways than one but judging by the tactics of the gray wolf lately, I think it would be best just to set him loose on this one."

Chapter 22

Pig addressed me. "This is a seventeen-shot Smith and Wesson 40 caliber handgun and the one holster is a twin. That's thirty-four shots in total. You are wearing my vest, and I would like it back please, holes and all. Don't worry about the car being seen, I'll take care of that after the fact. Focus and Uncle D are already in position to take the shipment. They are set to strike on sight, but we must draw my boys away from that area. It's 3 am and we have a small window. Are you ready?"

"Yeah, Pig."

"Listen, Prince, after tonight the heat will be on the gray from here on out."

"I know Pig, but I'm more afraid of my mother finding out."

"Don't trip Prince, we got you."

"Ok. Let's move then."

I climbed into the trunk of the black Audi. I had my gray uniform on with a 2-layered vest under it. There was a strap on the front of the vest holding the extra gun just in case. Focus thought it would be a fine idea to put gray paint on my face along with contacts to dull the description. Pig gave me a walkie-talkie to communicate with him on. We started on Pennsylvania and Dolphin in front of the mini market.

"Prince, come in!"

I pulled out the walkie, "Yeah pig!"

"Black Colombian jacket in front of the store on your left one minute. I will meet you on Preston Street and McCulloh in the lot."

"I hear you Pig."

"Go now, Prince!"

Once I stuffed the walkie back into my pocket, I swung the trunk up and jumped out running to my left with the 40 in my right hand. Two guys took off through the split toward the projects. Luckily, my target had a late reaction. Pig turned right up Dolphin Street before I shot the guy twice in his chest and then in his forehead as he slid down the wall. There were cars at the intersection but fuck it. I took off up Dolphin Street and hit a hard right through the court before I got to McCulloh. I cleared the projects in no time, hitting the split on the left which led me into the parking lot on W. Preston Street. I scanned the lot for Pig. He flashed his lights, and I jumped back into the trunk. I caught my breath while he drove. I already knew the area because we spent an hour scouting it before we started. Even though I was an outsider, West Baltimore was my hood tonight.

"Aye Prince!"

Once again, I grabbed the walkie, "Wuss up?!"

"Peek out the trunk, we are on McMechen Street coming up onto Dru Hill. Do you see the apartments on your right?"

"Yeah, Pig!"

"There's an alley on the side of them and that's where I'll be. Now to your left is a Safeway in the shopping center next to a small apartment complex. There're a few niggas standing in front of it. Clear them out! When I make this right on Dru Hill, jump out."

"I got you Pig!" I felt us turning and he shouted, "Go!"

I tucked the walkie and popped out of the trunk running towards the crowd. One of them yelled, "Oh shit!"

They all took off in different directions. Most of them ran into the complex but I knew better than that, so I chased a few of them over to the shopping center. I heard gunshots behind me. Suddenly I was running alongside the motherfuckers I was chasing. Then the unthinkable happened. An unmarked police car pulled into the parking lot behind us while the boys were still shooting. Two of them jumped out and one took off to chase the shooter. I hit the deck like I was shot, rolling back and forth screaming. The 40 was tucked under my left arm but my right hand was still palming it. The black Audi came through the alley and across the street. It was now or never. The officer got on his walkie while moving towards me. "I got a black male gray sweat suit and black tennis shoes. Possible gunshot victim.

Need an ambulance ASAP on MeMechen Street and Dru Hill in the shopping center lot."

He approached me. "Hold on man, where are you shot? Let me see buddy, maybe I can help."

When he kneeled, I rolled into him and pulled him towards me with my left hand. I whipped the gun from my armpit and placed it into his vest then opened fire. I emptied the entire clip into him at close range until I heard the gun click. I wanted to be sure that I pierced his vest. He fell on top of me, forcing me to crawl from under him. I was covered in blood and by instinct, I took his walkie and ran towards Pig. He was standing outside of the car in the alley in shock as I got closer.

"Get in the car Pig!"

"What the fuck Prince!"

"Get in and pull off!"

I jumped into the trunk, and he took off. There was blood in my mouth and inside of my clothes. It was a sticky feeling, but my adrenaline was racing so fast, I didn't care.

"Pig came through my radio immediately.

"Prince!"

"Yeah, Pig wuss up?"

"Are you hit, baby boy?"

"No, but I do look like a tampon back here."

"Thank the lord! Thia would've had our nuts behind you boy!"

"Pig, I would be in more trouble than everybody if this shit went south," August replied.

"You're done for the night, Prince, fuck that!" Pig insisted.

Meanwhile, the partner of the wounded cop called in the incident: "Officer down! Officer down! We have a narcotics UC down in the parking lot of the Safeway on McMechen and Dru Hill Over!"

"This is dispatch officer identify yourself."

"Officer Graham Wade, badge #1612 narcotics division, western district! My partner Lt. Marvin Curtis is suffering multiple gunshot wounds to the torso and abdomen. Suspect is not in sight, please send all units!"

“Sending the cavalry officer Wade to dispatch out.”

As I listened to the police radio, I hit Pig.

“Let Focus know it’s about that time! If this ain’t a good diversion, then I don’t know what is!”

“I just texted them, Prince, it’s on!”

Chapter 23

Uncle D got back into the car.

"That's the last of the lights."

"I can see that," Focus replied.

"Pig said they usually park and leave the shipment. That means they must have a car nearby watching the transaction," Uncle D insisted.

Focus replied, "Well, there's only one parking space open, and that's about 20ft ahead."

"If they're stuck in routine then they won't expect us. That's why killing the lights was so imminent," Uncle D added.

"Anyway, how's the "Queen" doing?"

Focus cut his eye at him and said, "Don't get me started; she's a handful and so headstrong!"

"Remind you of someone?" Uncle D asked.

"I know, right? I'm just glad I didn't have a son. She fights a lot and I think she likes girls," Focus revealed.

"Thia would put things in perspective for her."

"Soon D, she needs more time.

Suddenly multiple police cars swept down the street, horns blaring. A helicopter followed soon after.

"There goes our diversion. They're heading towards the North Avenue area.

"I see that, but where's the shipment?" Uncle D inquired.

"They'll be here," Focus insisted.

After a few moments, Uncle D received a text message. He let out a heavy chuckle that caught Focus' attention.

"The Prince hit a cop and got away too!" Uncle D informed.

"He better getaway, we trained him!" Focus replied.

After they shared a brief moment of triumph, Uncle D exposed the plot.

"Do you see that truck parked next to the space?

"I do," Focus replied.

I need you to hide under it, while I wait in the corner of the building near the alley."

"We need to be fast D. They should leave the keys in the van, so you just take it, and I will tail you," Focus instructed.

Without another word, they both exited the car and got into position. Within minutes, the officers eased down the street and pulled in front of the building.

"What the fuck happened to the lights?" one of the officers asked.

"Who knows, I'll call them to move this thing along. We got a call concerning a fellow officer in progress!" The superior officer replied.

Uncle D crept from the shadows, while signaling Focus to move in. Focus crawled from beneath the truck and pulled his Swiss blade from his pocket. The cop on his side rested his arm along the window as he smoked his cigarette. Uncle D grabbed the cop's forearm and snatched it backward, breaking it in half against the window. Before the cop could scream, Uncle D took hold of his throat and squeezed his trachea.

"Ambush!" The driver shouted as he turned to Uncle D. As he reached for his gun, Focus threw his arm around the cop's upper body and pulled him through the window.

"This is not a drill!" Focus taunted.

He then jammed the blade into the side of the officer's skull. He snatched it back out and plunged it into his head again before he twisted it to end him. Uncle D ripped the other cop from the car and slammed him onto the sidewalk. Uncle D held him down and rammed his knee into the man's jaw.

"The keys are in the ignition! Put him in the back and get a move on!" Focus commanded.

"What a lovely gift," Uncle D taunted as he slid the side door open and placed the cop onto the crates. He took his service weapon before he shut the door. Afterward, he hopped in the driver's seat and pulled off behind Focus. They made their way across town without incident. I was sitting on the couch back in the den when Pig received the call.

"Alright, hit me when you're close," Pig said before he hung up.

"Mission accomplished," He added as he looked at me.

"So I heard."

A few moments later, his phone began to ring, which meant they were there. Pig and I made our way to the door with haste. As we came out, we spotted the caravan pulling up slowly. Luzerne Street was clear of activity. Uncle D slid the door open as we approached him. There were two bodies on top of three wooden crates. The seats were removed for obvious reasons. Both Uncle D and Focus moved the bodies as we took the crates. Once we made it inside, Focus shouted, "We'll see you in a minute!"

I laid the crate down and ran to lock the door behind him. Afterward, Pig and I unloaded the guns and sorted them by size. We had a dozen of just about everything from pistols to rifles. Focus and Uncle D finally joined us as we were finishing up. Focus began to clap when he saw the arsenal. After they examined everything, Focus and Pig started packing it back into the crates. Uncle D and I took a seat on the sofa. He studied his nephew before he asked the obvious.

"Why did you "do" the cop, Prince?"

Everyone stopped their movements anticipating my answer.

"I couldn't get to the car without making Pig hot. I couldn't run with the crowd because I didn't know the area. So, I took my chance with the lone cop."

"He delivered an Oscar-worthy performance and convinced the officer that he was shot!" Pig added.

"You know this kind of shit doesn't happen, right?" Uncle D stated.

"Yeah, they will scorch the earth for your little ass!" Focus taunted.

I just figured it would be nice to clip one of them instead of our own for once."

Everyone nodded in agreement.

"We'll finish up here, August, take yourself home!" Focus ordered. I stood up and started toward the door.

"You rinsed yourself off, but you still have the DNA all over you. Watch yourself crossing the street and take the back door!" He added.

"Later, Pig!" I said.

"Later on, Little Prince!" Pig replied with a salute.

Before I could reach the stairs, my Uncle asked me, "Our cause determines?"

"The Qarma!" I replied.

"As greatness comes grateful to?"

"The Group!"

When I made it into the house, I stood under the shower for an hour. My mind was at ease for the most part, but the reality of the dead cop was a whole new cross to bear.

I had become what the fraternity had entrenched within me from the very moment I could think for myself.

"Lord knows I'm committed, but Heaven knows if I'll be forgiven."

***

Stay tuned for Part 2 to be released in the near future!